GHOSTLY PASSAGE

(A Joanna Davis Mystery)

R.K. O'Brien

ALL RIGHTS RESERVED

No part of this book may be reproduced or transmitted in any form or by any means, electronic or mechanical, including photocopying, recording, or by any information storage and retrieval system, without permission in writing from the author, except in the case of brief quotations embodied in reviews.

Copyright 2022 Rosemary O'Brien

Dedication:

To Alan, Nicholas and Alexander

Contents

Chapter 1 1

Chapter 2 5

Chapter 3 15

Chapter 4 22

Chapter 5 30

Chapter 6 43

Chapter 7 49

Chapter 8 56

Chapter 9 72

Chapter 10 86

Chapter 11 98

Chapter 12 110

Chapter 13 121

Chapter 14 131

Chapter 15 150

Chapter 16 159

Chapter 17 172

Chapter 18 178

Chapter 19 193

Chapter 20 211

Acknowledgements 216

CHAPTER 1

There was that noise again, the rhythmic tapping coming from the back of the room. The sound would sometimes continue for almost a half an hour and then stop suddenly, as suddenly as it started. There was no rhyme nor reason to it. She had asked the maintenance guys who once came in to fix an air conditioning problem, but they had informed her there was nothing marked on the blueprints behind that wall in that area of the library. She even pushed for an exterminator to go through the building and they found nothing other than little field mice, but they were outside. There was no rodent activity in the actual building.

The issue was that it was happening more frequently lately. Perhaps the uptick was because of the time of year. May was when the kids were finishing their school year by studying for exams and those who were heading to college were also figuring out how to pay for that privilege. Most of them were high school students, but the little ones often came in with their parents to pick out books and wandered into the Reference Room to look around. Celine often saw parents using it as a quiet place to look through the newspaper or a magazine while their little one perused one of the books they had just checked out in the Children's Room of the building.

Right now it was too early for those other than the staff to be here because the library was not open yet. This was often when the noises were most active. It was as if whatever it was didn't want anyone other than Celine to know they were there. Because Celine

Ghostly Passage

definitely had a feeling the noises were caused by a 'they,' or something intelligent like a spirit or ghost of some sort.

Celine believed in ghosts. She had a grandmother who was very sensitive to otherworldly phenomena. Granny knew ahead of time when people were going to die, she claimed to have been able to 'see' or 'hear' people who had already passed, and even claimed the family home she lived in until she died was haunted by her brother Anthony. She looked crazy when she would lift her head slightly and smile as if she were listening to something, something no one else could hear. When Celine once asked her about it, she said her brother was around and it made her smile. And it wasn't as if she were heading down the road of dementia. She did this even when she was younger and her children still lived home. Her brother had died when Granny was a teenager. Anthony was a couple of years older and got into a terrible car accident with his buddies. No one knew all the details, but Anthony had a run-in with a carriage horse on the street and was trampled. It was a comfort to her grandmother when he began appearing to her. She said Anthony told her he died instantly and that's all Granny wanted to know. It brought her comfort he had not suffered.

So, Celine was sure the rhythmic tapping was something trying to get a message out now that she had disproven the physical possibilities such as jiggling pipes or some sort of problem with the wiring, not that that would have made noise.

The sound continued as Celine straightened up the magazines. She could still hear it on the other side of the library where she found a folded newspaper on a table in the back of the bookcases. She placed it on the top of the pile of recent issues of the New Haven Registers she kept and went to investigate.

As she walked closer, the tapping got louder. She was not going crazy; she knew it was really happening. Just as she got about a foot away from the wall, she almost went through the roof from fright.

"Hello Celine!" Donna from the Children's Room was suddenly behind her. "I'm sorry! I didn't mean to startle you," she said. "I just wanted to let you know I will be giving a tour for the Fifth Graders today."

Celine had her hand on her chest as if calming her heartbeat that rambled in her chest after that surprise.

"No worries," she replied, her rapid breathing contradicting her words. "I just didn't hear you come in, that's all."

"What were you doing anyway? You looked as if you were creeping up on something."

Celine had not told anyone about the tapping other than the maintenance man, Steve, in charge of the building. She didn't want anyone to think she was losing her mind. Even Steve didn't know the whole story. She wanted to keep it that way.

"Oh, I just thought I saw a bug or something," Celine said. "I think it was just a piece of lint."

"Okay," Donna said, already turning away. "I just wanted to give you a heads up. I'll be bringing them by around 11:00. We're going to do the usual and visit the Adult Section, here and then I think they're going to lunch somewhere."

"Fun," Celine replied. "An end-of-the-year field trip to fill out the year. Thanks for letting me know."

"No problem," Donna said and left the room.

"That's enough of that," Celine muttered to herself as she resolved to do something about this tapping once and for all. She wouldn't wait for Joanna to visit. She would email her. Celine regularly helped her with her research. Maybe Joanna could use her newly discovered medium skills to help her this time. It was worth a try.

Celine went to her computer and started composing the email. She worded it carefully, proofread it and hit the send button, hoping Joanna would not mind the imposition.

CHAPTER 2

Felix walked with Joanna from the kitchen as she went to her office to begin her day. As she set down her coffee, he sniffed around her office before settling on the couch she kept along one wall. He liked the fluffy pillows she kept there in case she wanted to edit an article she worked on or read a book. She liked to be cozy while she worked and occasionally when she read someone else's book.

"Are you getting cozy for the day you lazy thing?" Joanna scratched the back of Felix's neck and listened to his loud purr. It was as if chocolate had a sound and his purring always put her to sleep when he jumped into bed at night. He seemed happy that neither the workmen who had been working on her house renovations nor the resident ghost was around anymore. Felix was the one who had alerted her to Sophia, the ghost who began Joanna's reluctant journey as a medium. Felix's hissing every time he saw her kept her from being ignored. Thank goodness her actual murderer was about to be sentenced. Tommy, the man who took the blame initially, was finally free now that Squirrel had received a guilty verdict. Joanna did not know what kind of compensation Tommy might receive, but she hoped it was something. He had been in jail for 18 years for a crime he did not commit.

Joanna took a sip of her coffee and wandered into the den, pondering how a killer could have ended up working on her house. He painted the upstairs bathroom and worked on the fireplace in her den. He did beautiful work, she thought as she gazed at the stonework he carefully repaired. From the way Tommy told the story to Detective Sosa at the time of Sophia's murder, Tommy didn't have much going for him. He was homeless, his family was gone, and he was constantly drunk. As such, he could not hold down a job. Couch surfing at Squirrel's was a regular occurrence because of their high school friendship. Squirrel felt bad for him. When Squirrel went into a black rage at Sophia's house and whacked her with a shovel as she turned away, Tommy decided to take the blame for the murder and Squirrel let him.

What a piece of dirt, Joanna thought, turning away from the fireplace and making her way back to her desk. She turned on her computer and clicked on her email. It was a thirty-minute task at the beginning of each workday so she did not let thousands of emails pile up during the course of the week. Since it was Thursday, she had been through the process several times already that week resulting in only about 300 emails. Most were junk, but one stood out.

Joanna clicked on an email from Celine at the West Haven Public Library. She rarely reached out to her in any manner, but Joanna saw her regularly when she visited the Reference Room. The Internet was obviously her usual way to research information for the books or articles she wrote, but sometimes Joanna preferred a visit to the actual library. Paper books still held an allure for her as she was a bookworm from way back. She loved walking to the library with her friend Laura when she was in elementary school. They would visit the Children's Room, pick out a few books, then she and Laura would grab a soda before walking back home with their treasures after sitting on the Green to chat and drink their drinks.

Upon clicking open Celine's email, Joanna was surprised. Celine thought she had a ghost in the Reference Room. She wanted Joanna to come in as soon as possible and let her know what she thought about it. Having been a part of solving Sophia's murder, Celine felt Joanna had some more insight than Celine ever could and just wanted her thoughts on what she might be able to do about it if it was, indeed, some sort of haunting.

Joanna almost choked on the swig of coffee she had just swallowed. She had never wanted to acknowledge her gift of being able to see, hear and talk to souls who had passed. Sophia, the ghost, had simply plagued her with visits until Joanna could no longer avoid it. She had even gone to the police after she gathered enough information. Luckily the first detective she dealt with was a believer in all of that supernatural stuff. He humored her until it became apparent that there was something to the evidence she kept showing up with. His chat with Tommy in jail had been the turning point of the entire situation, but Joanna had never wanted to do any of this. She had denied her apparent gift since she was ten years old until it became obvious she had to do something for Sophia's memory or else live with a ghost who frequently badgered her while she made dinner or even when she slept. After a number of four a.m. wake up calls from banging in her kitchen or hissing from her cat, she had to act at the time. Now Sophia rested again and so did Joanna.

Until now. Joanna had gotten a bit of notoriety around West Haven for her gifts despite the nasty gossips who could not refrain from slamming her reputation, but she had gotten through it and moved past that. Now she was once again the author who lived in town, but now with the added ingredient of being a medium, whether she wanted to or not.

Joanna did not give readings to anyone or anything like that, but the community knew all about the case and either thought it was interesting having someone 'like that' in the community or enjoyed gossiping about it. She suspected the latter but didn't really care anymore. People were always going to look for something to do when they had no lives, and the gossips definitely had no lives to speak of. They accomplished nothing, they put nothing useful into the community, and often were jealous of those who did, like Joanna. Her five bestselling novels and thriving content writing business made her a successful person in their eyes. Joanna was just trying to make a living and enjoy her life like everyone else.

A visit to the library was always fun for Joanna. She responded to Celine's email and set about to finish her most important tasks for the day and visit later in the afternoon. If nothing else, she was curious to find out what was going on in the building she loved.

Joanna parked on Elm St., down the street from the entrance. The walk up to the West Haven Public Library at this time of year was always lovely. A few flowering pear trees along the way combined with the trees full of green, new leaves gave Joanna a sense of calm and hope for the world, even if the world frequently disappointed her. It was always this way for her. She loved when the trees flowered and branched out in the spring. It gave her a temporary sense of well-being. Joanna seemed to remember hearing something about another city making a gift of the trees many years ago. Regardless, they were around as long as Joanna could remember. She made a note to look up that little bit of information. Perhaps she would be able to use it in a story one day.

The door to the library opened before Joanna reached it and revealed Mrs. Sasso, a librarian she had dealt with many times.

"Hello, Joanna! What a pleasure to run into you!" she said.

"Hey there, Mrs. Sasso."

"Are you working on anything interesting these days? I thought I heard something about a new book about what happened last year," she said, her eyes bright with curiosity.

"Well, why not, right?" Joanna said, happy to walk about her work with a true reader devoid of gossiping tendencies. "The story literally fell into my lap!"

Joanna had decided to try a new genre, a mystery this time. She usually wrote middle of the road women's fiction and stayed away from romance, but this story truly landed in her lap. She figured she would tweak the facts here and there to make it more interesting and, of course, leave the real names out of the book.

"I assume you're going to make it more interesting here and there, right? You know, kind of spice up the parts that aren't necessarily interesting," Mrs. Sasso correctly supposed.

"Yes, we'll see how it presents itself," Joanna responded taking a step closer to the door. "Right now I'm only in the outlining stage."

"That's probably the fun part where you see what the story can be, right?"

"Absolutely," she said. "After you figure out the stumbling blocks you can just write. The fun part for me."

"Well, I'll let you go, but we'll have to have you speak at the library at some point soon," Mrs. Sasso said, turning to leave. She turned back briefly. "I would love to have a talk about your process. It's glamourous to those of us who love books, but don't write for a living!"

"I'd be happy to visit," Joanna said, reaching for the handle of the door. "Just email me and let me know when you want to put me on the schedule."

"I will, Dear," she waved. "Have a good afternoon!" The enthusiastic librarian walked away.

"You, too!" Joanna said and pulled the door open to make her way to the Reference Room. It was four o'clock. Joanna went up the short staircase, opened another door and headed to the right. The Reference Room stood quiet, all of the students cramming for exams and people reading the newspapers the library had on hand.

"Hi, Celine," Joanna said, her voice soft to accommodate the quiet of the room. "How are you doing?"

Joanna's smile faded when she saw Celine's face. Celine held up one finger, pushed some papers into a pile to the side and motioned for Joanna to follow her out of the room and into the hallway.

"Uh, oh," Joanna grimaced. "What's going on? Are you okay?"

"Kind of," Celine responded. "I hate to bother you about this, but I know you've been exploring your psychic abilities, so I thought I would venture a request."

"As I said, uh, oh," Joanna replied. "Look, I'm not doing anything officially, just exploring things after that Squirrel and Tommy thing at my house." Joanna still didn't want to get visits from the 'other side,' but Celine looked desperate. To be honest, Joanna was intrigued and had to find out what was going on.

"Is this at your house?"

"No, here at the library," Celine whispered. "I don't look around much while there are patrons here, but after they leave, or before I open in the morning, stuff happens."

"What kind of stuff?" Joanna leaned in. She knew they were probably too quiet for anyone in the Reference Room to hear them, but you never knew.

"Knocking and tapping, mostly," she said. "Every now and then I'll find a newspaper moved from where I put it, but I figure maybe a patron did that, though when it happens, it doesn't seem possible."

"What do you mean?"

"Well, I'll see it left on one side of the table after everyone has left, then five minutes later after I do something on the other side of the room, I'll come back to it and see it on the other side of the table. It's weird."

"That sounds cool, though," Joanna grinned. "Where is this tapping happening? Is it in one place or all around the room?"

"No, it's in one place, at the back of that side room there," Celine said, pointing in the general direction of the back of the Reference Room.

Joanna's grin fell when she realized the reason Celine might be including her in on her secret.

"So, why are you telling me this, dare I ask?"

"I want you to investigate it," Celine said quietly. "I know it's a lot to ask and you don't really do this sort of thing…"

"I don't," Joanna interrupted.

"But I thought since you worked on that case about that woman's murder, I'd see if you could check this out, even in an informal investigation."

Celine's look was so full of hope, Joanna had a difficult time declining her request.

"The thing with Sophia happened accidentally. I didn't do anything to bring it on or anything," Joanna said, reluctant to commit fully.

Joanna remembered being scared to death when the ghost, Sophia, first showed up in her kitchen. The fact that she could see and hear her threw Joanna for a loop, but she could not get rid of her. The more she tried to ignore her, the more Sophia got into her head, asking her to help put away the person who murdered her. How could Joanna say no especially when Sophia kept haunting her and would not go away no matter how much Joanna ignored her 4am wake-up calls and late-night visits?

Celine stood in front of Joanna waiting for her final decision. Joanna sighed.

"OK, I'll look at it, but I really don't know what I can do about it if there is anything there," she said.

"Oh, thank you," Celine said, grabbing one of Joanna's hands and squeezing it. "I just want to know if there is anything haunting the library or if I'm hearing things."

"I'm not promising anything official, but I'll take a look," Joanna said. "Do you want me to come back when the library is closed or do you care if the patrons know what's going on?"

"Oh, no, I don't want them to know anything is going on, either the patrons or the staff!" Celine looked horrified at the thought. Joanna was quick to reassure her.

"Don't worry," Joanna jumped in. "I won't tell anyone." *Except probably the paranormal group Joanna was a member of, but Celine didn't need to know about her secret membership.*

"Can you come back tomorrow after the library closes at 5?" Celine asked. "Take my number and text me when you get here. I'll open the door. Make it 5:15 in case we have any stragglers. Does that work for you?"

"Perfect," Joanna responded, punching Celine's phone number in her cell. "I just called you so you would have my number, too."

"Great," Celine said, answering her phone when it rang and plugging Joanna into her phone contacts. "I would walk you back there now, but there are too many people back in that area right now. I don't want to alert anyone to anything."

"No problem, Celine," Joanna said. "I'll see you tomorrow evening at about 5:15." Joanna shook Celine's hand. "I'm not sure what I can do, but maybe I can confirm or deny your suspicions."

"I appreciate it!" Celine exclaimed. "I am losing my mind with this tapping and just want to know what might be going on."

"No worries," Joanna said, breaking away from Celine and moving toward the door. The librarian at the main desk in the Adult section looked a little too nosy for Joanna's taste, so she just winked at Celine and left the library.

Joanna walked back to her car hoping she didn't get herself into anything messy. What if she found some sort of spirit or ghost in the room? What was she supposed to do if that happened? She only helped the police department out when her good friend, Detective Sosa, called her, and it was a quiet thing. No one else knew, nothing was attributed to Joanna and she didn't do it often. That's the way she liked it. Nathan was a believer and Joanna was happy to help if no one else knew about her gifts, a gift she had denied firmly until Sophia's ghost came into her life. The last case he called about had been about a missing woman, believed to be murdered. They knew where she had lived, knew she was abducted from her home and probably killed, but there was no body. Joanna sat quietly, holding a scarf she wore often and the impressions came in clearly. The police were directed to a large, grassy area near the Long Island Sound in Branford where they found the unfortunate woman face down and bludgeoned to death. Joanna had not felt essential, but the police were happy to have a body and eventually solved the case. Her murderer was doing life in prison.

Clicking the button to unlock her car door, Joanna got in and drove home, wondering what she had just gotten herself into.

CHAPTER 3

"Yes, but she doesn't want anyone knowing I'm even looking around," Joanna argued to her paranormal group the next day. "In fact, I'm meeting her after the library closes for the day today so no one gets wind of anything unusual going on."

The paranormal group met on Saturdays at 2:00. She had found them when Sophia showed up at her house and Joanna needed to learn more about paranormal events. Since then, the group members had all become her friends. There was Anne, the group leader, who Joanna was closest to. Anne was a widow who lived by herself and had taken over when the previous leader, Patty, passed away a few years ago. Then there was Maria, a quiet middle-aged woman who heard spirits who had passed and was working on controlling it a bit better. Nick had been working on a story for the newspaper when he found the group. He joined because he had similar gifts as Maria and was happy to discover there were others like him. Sylvia, the quietest of the group, lived in an old house that was haunted, as many old houses are, and Laura, who was comfortable with her gifts and found the group while looking for likeminded people, somewhat like Joanna herself.

"Maybe she'll let us go in there now," Laura suggested.

"Absolutely not," Joanna protested. "I promised her confidentiality and I don't want to break that trust on the very first day."

"But we're a group that deals with that sort of thing," Nick said. "If not us, then who? Collectively I think we can help her figure out what's going on, don't you think?"

"I know what you're saying, but I don't want to scare her off," Joanna said. "I promised her I would meet her by myself and I want to do so, at least the first time."

"Fine," Laura said. "But let us know when we can join you, okay?"

"I'll let her know you're around to help. 'Promise."

Frankly, Joanna hoped for something interesting, but she wasn't going to think that way. She wanted to approach the noises scientifically, ruling out anything physical like squirrels or some sort of problem with the building's mechanics, though it seemed as if the library's maintenance folks had done that already.

The rest of the meeting was spent discussing this new development of a possible ghost haunting the library.

At 5:15, Joanna was sitting in her car in the side lot of the library and texted Celine she had arrived. When she walked up to the door, Celine let her in.

"If anyone sees us, because there are eyes everywhere in this town, we'll say you were meeting me for coffee or extra help with some project, okay?"

"Celine," Joanna protested. "I don't think anyone's watching the library. And if they were, I don't think they would think anything of it!"

"Perfect, that would me another excuse. You are driving me home because my car broke down," Celine said, walking Joanna up the stairs and to the Reference Room.

"I gotta say, you would make a good crime novelist with all of the backstory you come up with on the fly!" Joanna grinned.

"I just don't want to stir anything up while we figure this out," Celine said, leading Joanna to the back section to the left of the room.

The wall Celine pointed out was bare. There were no windows in this section of the library, so thoughts of acorns or tree pieces being blown against them by the wind were immediately ruled out. Joanna went up to the wall and stood about two inches from it. She didn't have a clue what she was doing, but she thought if there was something there, she might feel something like she did when Sophia had been haunting her house.

"What's behind this wall?" Joanna asked.

"The maintenance men said there was nothing behind it. Just empty space," Celine responded.

"Nothing at all?"

"Nope," Celine said. "Do you want to take a look?"

"Sure," Joanna responded and began following Celine out of the Reference Room to the main library where the Adult Section was housed. As they did, they came upon Anne, Nick and Laura whispering in the lobby by the front door.

"The library is closed," Celine said with her stern librarian voice usually used for children misbehaving in the quiet Reference Room.

"What are you guys doing here?" Joanna sputtered. "I told you to stay away for now."

"You know these people?" Celine exclaimed.

"Yes, I'm sorry," Joanna apologized. "These are a few members of a paranormal group of which I'm a member, the few who did not take my direction to stay away!" Joanna shot them all a pointed look as she said that.

"We're sorry," Anne said. "But we thought we could help you with your investigation."

"It's not an investigation…" Celine began.

"Don't worry," Joanna explained. "These are people who will keep your secret. We talk about the paranormal at our weekly meetings. They just want to help," she said shooting Anne a 'mom look.'

"You didn't lock the door, so we came in," Nick said. "I'm Nick."

"Right," Laura added. "I'm Laura. You really don't have to worry about us. We won't say a word to anyone. We're just interested."

Celine eyed them all with suspicion but decided to give them a chance. Maybe more heads would figure this out more efficiently.

"Okay, then," she said. "I'm Celine the Reference Librarian. I really don't want this to get out, whatever it is. My boss doesn't even know I've asked Joanna to look into it."

"The same goes for me," Joanna said. "I don't want people to know I'm part of a paranormal group and I don't think these folks want their names out either."

"Fair enough," Celine said and led them to a wall in the main library. "She would think I was absolutely batty if she found out, so please keep it to yourself."

"We all get it," Joanna said. "Imagine what I went through with the stuff at my house? Because I'm somewhat known around here, people couldn't help but add their opinion. It's not fun."

"Yeah, don't worry," Nick added. "Our lips are sealed."

Just then Celine stopped at the wall behind the Reference Room.

"See? There's nothing here, just another wall."

"That's odd," Joanna said. "I would think the builders would have used the space rather than leave it empty."

"From what I remember about the history of this place, this main library was built onto the back of the Reference Room, right?" Anne asked.

"Yes, the Reference Room was the original library building," Celine responded, turning to lead them back into the Reference Room. "This entire room was part of the original building. They seemed to incorporate it into the new addition, but without any sort of plan from what I can tell. That was pretty common in the 1960's when the addition was built."

The group stood in the middle of the room with perplexed expressions.

"Do I sound crazy?" Celine asked. "I sound crazy," she reiterated. "I'm sure I'm wasting your time, though I really only asked for Joanna's time."

"Will you forgive us?" Anne said. "We really do want to help and this will give us fodder for our next meeting."

"No problem," Celine said. "Just keep me updated if you think of anything and keep this to yourselves, please."

"We will, and I ask you to do the same regarding our little group," Joanna responded.

"No problem," Celine answered.

"Thank you for confiding in me about this. It may be nothing, but we'll figure it out," Joanna assured the skittish librarian.

"Thank you," she said. "And now I need to let you out if you're not going to do anymore investigating tonight." Celine led them out of the Reference Room and back to the front door. "It's been a long day."

The group apologized again and left the building while Celine locked up. They all stood in the side parking lot discussing what they just heard which was actually nothing much.

"Well, we're not going to figure it out here, so let's think about it and talk again at our meeting next Saturday," Anne said. "Joanna, can we get into the Reference Room earlier if we need to?"

"I'm sure Celine will let me in and maybe you like she did today, but please, everyone, promise me you won't just go in and look around without me or during an official group visit, okay? I don't want to get her in trouble or scare her off from investigating," Joanna pleaded.

Heartfelt apologies and agreements followed until they all got into their cars and left. They would be back next week for their paranormal group meeting but each promised to email the group if anyone thought of anything new or helpful before that.

Meanwhile, Celine walked through the library making sure lights were turned off, locking the main door behind her again. She hoped she wasn't starting anything that would get her in trouble, but she simply had to find an answer to that stupid knocking before it drove her crazy!

Celine came out of the library. "Thanks Joanna," she said. "I hope this isn't an inconvenience. I live in the West Shore area and really appreciate the ride."

"No problem at all, Celine," Joanna replied, guiding Celine to her car. The drive to Celine's house was quick and they had a nice conversation on the way.

"Thanks again, Joanna," Celine said before shutting the door and letting herself in to her house. Joanna hoped the paranormal folks honored Celine's wishes and did not bust in to one of these library investigations again. They were helpful, though. Maybe she could talk Celine into allowing their visits.

CHAPTER 4

When Joanna opened the door to her house, she was greeted by the roar of Italian curse words and the intermittent sound of a chain saw. Sal, her contractor, was back at work at her house to do more work, this time unplanned. In March, a Nor'easter blew in with high winds that caused one of the old trees in her backyard to fall onto the back of her house. Luckily it had not hit her new bathroom, completed by this same crew last year, but it damaged the roof above her spare room. She was not happy about this development at all but knew she could not have a hole in her roof if she was to keep her house in shape. The first bad storm would fill it with water.

Joanna had bought out her ex-husband when they got divorced a few years ago and was working on making it her own. Since her books started taking off with generous advances from the publisher, she had a nice nest egg with which to do the renovations. The first renovation had been on her kitchen. That had been when she found Sal through word-of-mouth. She trusted him and his crew despite the small matter of the stone mason/painter who had turned out to be a murderer. It had been a surprise to all of them, his coworkers and friends included, since he passed his background check with Sal. The deed had only been revealed through Sophia, the ghost in Joanna's kitchen, but that was a whole other matter.

Next, Joanna had them renovate her upstairs bathroom installing a huge antique claw-footed tub she had discovered in a New York

City salvage company. It was during the next project while they were working on updating her den that it was revealed Sal's stone mason who worked on her fireplace and painted her upstairs bathroom, had murdered one of Joanna's neighbors many years ago. His friend took the blame and Squirrel, that was what people called him, got off Scot free with no one any wiser.

Joanna loved all three rooms and had planned on waiting to do any more work until the tree made the decision for her.

She dropped her purse in her office off the entrance to the house and followed the swearing up the stairs. There she found sawhorses covered in wood that Rob was cutting with the electric chain saw. He turned it off and lifted his safety glasses as she walked in.

"Hey, Ms. Davis!" he said, a big smile on his face. "What's going on?"

"That's what I was wondering about when I heard the commotion," she said, her eyes scanning the heavy cracks in the corner of the ceiling.

"It's no problem," Sal said, giving Mario the side-eye. "Mario here just needs a little encouragement to keep his swearing to a minimum."

"I'm sorry, Joanna," he said, leaning the heavy lumber he had been balancing on a should against the wall. "I hope I didn't bother you."

"Not at all, Mario," she said, completely at ease with him using her first name. "And, Rob, call me Joanna, please. You make me feel like a schoolmarm when you call me Ms. Davis. We're around the same age after all."

"I know," Rob said, "I'll try, but you're technically my boss…after Sal, that is," he quickly corrected himself.

"Just try," Joanna smiled. "I promise you won't burst into flames or anything if you do."

"No problem," he said.

"Do you need anything else?" Sal asked directing his question to her.

"No, I'm good," she said. "I got home a few minutes ago and wanted to check on you guys. 'Everything good? Do you need anything like coffee or water or anything?" Joanna always asked, they always declined, but it was a habit to ask people in her home if they needed any refreshment, even if they did work for her.

"No, we're all good," the three men said in a chorus. They paused before laughing at their unintended chorus. "We're almost done here. 'Sorry we're here so late in the day." It was already six thirty.

"No worries," she said. "I guess none of you have any hot dates or anything."

"Nah, we're a bunch of old married people. I wanted to finish up something, but we'll be out of here in a few minutes," Sal responded to her back while the chain saw resumed its cacophony.

When she got downstairs, Joanna walked into her kitchen to look around for something to make for dinner. Felix jumped up on the counter to say, "Hello."

"How are you my fuzzy friend?" Joanna said, greeted with a purr in response to the rub to his head she gave him. "You're not supposed to be on the counter you bad boy." The cat looked at her as if to say, "Whatever. I'm cute."

Joanna lifted Felix off the counter before opening the refrigerator to scour ingredients and leftovers for her possible supper. She had some leftover lentil soup, some chicken and rice that she put away in a neat container so she could easily heat it in the microwave, and she had the usual salad fixings. Maybe she would add some cheese and have a tossed salad. While she was gazing into the fridge, the guys walked past her. She stood up and closed the door.

"We'll see you on Monday," Sal said, bringing up the rear.

"Have a good Sunday, Joanna," Rob said with a smile.

" 'You see? You didn't burst into flames!" she said, smiling at Rob.

"I know, but it's weird," he said.

"You'll get used to it, right Mario?"

"Right, Joanna!" he said, slapping Rob on the shoulder in front of him and walking through the back door.

"What a bunch of clowns," Sal said, waving and closing the door behind him.

Joanna smiled. She knew she was lucky to have found such a competent and genial group of workers to fix up her house. Sal was the best and they all knew what they were doing from what Joanna could tell. Her kitchen, bathroom and den were just the way she wanted them now that they finished construction and she had decorated to her taste.

Ghostly Passage

Joanna turned back to the fridge, pondering her choices for her evening meal. She would have a salad and leftovers. She had just popped the leftover chicken and rice into the microwave and started on making a salad when the phone rang. She reached over to pick it up and saw it was her daughter, Julia.

"Hi, Honey!" she said, delighted to hear from her. "No hot date tonight?"

"Not tonight, Mom," she sighed. "I went out to dinner with a few friends last night, but tonight I'm staying home with a good book."

"Oh, yeah? 'Sounds comfy. What are you reading?" Joanna asked.

"I don't remember the title, but it's downloaded on my tablet," she responded. "It has something to do with the French resistance during World War II. It's an historical novel."

"I never remember the titles either," Joanna said. "Isn't that awful? I should remember at least the author, but I never do."

"As long as it's good. Besides, I can look at my purchase history to see what I like anyway."

"That's true," Joanna said while she absently chopped tomatoes to toss into her salad.

"Oh, and I have some sad news for you," Julia began.

"What happened?" Joanna exclaimed. "Did someone die?"

"Yes, Tommy."

"What?!" Joanna shouted into the phone. "What happened? And why didn't Sal tell me? I saw him today."

"Maybe he hasn't heard about it yet," Julia said. "It just came across my news feed five minutes ago. I have an alert for that story."

"Wow, I'll have to look when I get off the phone. What happened?" Joanna asked, her salad abandoned for the moment.

"The story says he couldn't cope outside of jail," Julia explained. "He hung himself in the halfway house he was living in in New Haven."

"That's so sad," Joanna said. "I wonder how Squirrel feels about that?"

"Yeah, he basically killed a second person, if they were the only two people he murdered in his life," Julia said, disdain dripping from her words.

"No, I don't think he killed anyone else, at least according to Detective Sosa." Sosa had worked on the case after Joanna had gone to him with her 'psychic' information from beyond the grave. Nathan Sosa chalked the murder up to a one-time crime of passion.

"Let's hope he's right," Julia said. "Okay, so with that news, my food delivery is here. Gotta go."

"Okay, Honey. Enjoy your book!" Joanna said.

"And you have a good night, too," Julia said and hung up.

It was already 7:30 when Joanna put down her phone, so she finished preparing her salad, took her dinner plate out of the microwave and went to the den in search of a good movie. She had just settled on a documentary that looked promising and had taken one bite of her salad when her cell phone rang again.

"Hello?" she said between swallows of her tomato.

Ghostly Passage

"Hey, there, it's Anne," was the reply on the other end of the line. "I hope I'm not bothering you. You sound as if you're eating."

"I am, but that's okay," Joanna said, hitting PAUSE on the TV remote. "What's up?"

"I'll make this quick, then," she said. "What if we got approval to poke a hole in that wall just to see what is behind it?"

"Do you think we can? That sounds difficult in such an old building, no?" Joanna said, surprised, but intrigued by the idea.

"Well, I know someone on the Library Board and may be able to quietly ask instead of making it a whole City issue."

"I don't see why not. I would imagine if you found a sympathetic ear, they would be as curious as we are to know what's behind that wall."

"That's what I thought, but how do I approach it without telling them about the reasons for our little investigation? Any ideas?" Anne added.

"We can come up with a story that doesn't implicate Celine if that's what she prefers," Joanna suggested.

"I figured that's what she would prefer. She seems kind of skittish about it all."

"Skittish, yes, but definitely a believer in things beyond, so to speak," Joanna replied. "Why don't you see what you can do on Monday? For now, just enjoy your weekend, but I think it's a good idea. We have to see what's back there."

"Okay, I'll call my contact on Monday," Anne said. "Until then, have a good weekend and sorry to interrupt your meal."

"That's no problem at all," Joanna said. "I'll talk to you during the week."

As Joanna munched on her dinner, she thought about what could be behind that wall. And why wasn't there a door or some sort of entrance in that space? It was odd, she thought, as she hit 'play' on her remote and enjoyed her late dinner, the news about Tommy and library temporarily pushed to the back of her thoughts, or at least to the side for a while.

CHAPTER 5

On Tuesday, Sal had barely come in the house when he stopped Joanna as she moved to the coffee maker.

"Oh my God, did you hear?" he said, his excitement obvious, but not a good kind of excitement. Joanna was sure he was talking about Tommy, so she just frowned and nodded.

"I can't believe it, can you?" Sal said. Mario and Rob were filing in just then, listening with interest.

"Well, we never know why someone commits suicide," she said, pulling her cup out from under the drip and taking a sip. "It's so sad, though."

"Yeah, but he had just gotten his freedom after all these years," Mario said, pulling up alongside Sal. "Wouldn't that make you want to stay around a while?"

"Maybe he couldn't take the outside world after being locked up all that time," Rob added, walking past the little group and heading to the front of the house. "He probably couldn't deal with all of the new stuff that he wasn't used to, right?" Rob said. "It is sad, though," he added. "I'm heading upstairs to set up." With that, he was done with the conversation.

"It's gloomy," Joanna agreed. "He had no time to do anything with his life except sit in a cell for someone else's crime."

"How did you find out?" Sal asked. "Did that detective call you?"

"No, my daughter had a notice come through her newsfeed the other night," Joanna responded.

"My wife heard it on the local news Sunday," Mario said. "It really is terrible, especially since we all went to school with him around the same time."

"I wonder what Squirrel is thinking right now?" Sal said, shaking his head. The three stood there in silence for a few moments thinking about what a loser Squirrel was before Sal broke up the reverie.

"We should get started," Sal said nodding Mario out of the kitchen.

"Okay, let me know if you need anything," Joanna said, as she followed them to the front of her house and went into her office to start the day. She opened her email and the first one that caught her eye was from Anne. Joanna opened it and read that Anne had gotten permission from her friend on the library board to cut a small hole in the wall just to see what was behind it. Joanna immediately called Anne.

"Wow!" she said when Anne picked up on the first ring.

"Right? I guess you got my email."

"I did and I'm so excited to hear this," Joanna exclaimed. "Who is this benevolent soul?"

"His name is Buddy Lawson and I actually went to elementary school with him."
"That's helpful. Do you want me to call Celine and tell her?"

"I already did and she's expecting us on Thursday night after the library closes," Anne said. "The only problem is we need someone who'll cut the wall without spreading the word around town."

"And you were thinking of my guy Sal for the job I bet," Joanna replied.

"Well, yes, I was," Anne said. Joanna could hear her smirking into the phone. "Do you think he will do it for us?"

"He may," Joanna said. "I'll wait until he's at lunch to ask him. They just started upstairs and I don't want to break the momentum."

"OK, well, text me when you know. Do you want me to tell the others?"

"No, let's just keep it between us for now, assuming Buddy is going to show up as well. That would make six people already. It's kind of a crowd."

"You're right. We can tell the paranormal group on Saturday if we find anything," Anne said. "For now, I'll let you get on with your day."

"Okay," Joanna said. "Thanks for doing this. It's going to be interesting, I hope."

"Said by the woman who didn't want to get involved!" Anne laughed. "I'll talk to you later."

"Okey doke," Joanna said, smiling as she clicked out of the call. The next email was from a client accepting her revisions on a story about the metaverse. Joanna was still trying to figure out what exactly that was and was happy to research and write the article.

The day moved forward until she heard Sal and his crew walking by her office.

"We'll be out in the yard, Joanna," Sal said through the open door as he walked by.

"Can you come in here for a minute, Sal?"

"Uh, oh," he said. "What happened now?" Joanna's house always had something to fix, so Sal was weary of another project to put on his schedule. It was heading toward summer and he had a lot of work on the books right now.

"It's nothing bad," she said, seeing his face.

"Good," he said and stepped into the office.

"Can you close the door?" she said, noting the troubled look reappear on his face.

"Are you sure nothing's wrong?" he said, closing the door behind him.

"Promise," she said. "Do you know about the library issue that came up this weekend?"

"What, do they need work, too? I'm kind of busy right now."

"Not exactly, just a quick job as a favor for me."

'What's going on?" he said, scooting over to take a seat on the couch. If she was asking for a favor, he could at least take a load off while he listened.

Joanna told him about the librarian's concerns about the Reference Room, the wall and the permission to open the wall a bit. He listened, nodded at her and started asking questions.

"Can we get this guy to write it down so I don't get into trouble with the city?" was his first question. He needed to preserve his reputation.

"I'm sure we can," she said. "He's a friend of one of the people investigating as well as a board member."

"When would this be?"

"She made an appointment for Thursday night, but it has to be after the library closes for the day so it doesn't draw attention to anything."

"What time Thursday?" he asked, pulling out his phone to look at his calendar. Joanna knew he often scheduled smaller jobs after he was done with her house or went to check on one of his other crews. He had two more aside from the one at her house. Plus he had a wife at home who liked to see him.

"So is 8:15 is good?" He knew the library closed at 8:00 because he sometimes took his grandchildren to the library for story time even if it was just his reading a book to them. He usually went during the day, but there was that occasional evening visit during the summer or holiday weeks.

"Perfect," Joanna responded. "And please don't tell anyone about this especially those two old ladies you work with." Mario and Rob had let everyone know about Joanna's ghost when she was helping Sophia and the whole town had something to say about it, both in person and through social media. She didn't want to start that up again.

"Promise," he said. "Is that it?"

"Yes, that's it for now," Joanna said.

"Have a good afternoon."

"Thanks, Sal. You too." Joanna turned back to her computer after she texted Anne with the time. Joanna had no idea how she got sucked into these things when she never wanted to use her gifts in the first place, but this *was* interesting. She wondered, like everyone else involved, why essentially an empty room would be built. The hole in the wall would surely bring some answers, she thought, getting back to the metaverse article.

Her curiosity, however, was not to be appeased on Thursday night. When she arrived, with Sal already waiting in his truck parked at the back of the parking lot away from the street's prying eyes, Celine was at the top of the stairs waiting for her.

"We have bad news, Joanna," she said, wringing her hands. "Hi, I'm Celine," she said, offering her hand to Sal.

"Sal," he said.

"What's the news?" Joanna asked, following Celine to the Reference Room. "There's someone here from City Council who doesn't want us to cut open the wall."

"Did you tell him why we're doing it? And wait. How did he or she find out anyway?"

"It's a 'she,' and I guess Mr. Lawson mentioned it when they met up for something. I don't think Lawson thought anything about it as any reasonable person might not."

Joanna shook her head as she entered the room. When she got back to that area of the room, she saw Lawson arguing with that woman Carol she had seen walking to the City Clerk's office last year. She was always someone who had to have her nose in everything from what she knew of her. She had been on the PTA when her kids were in school.

"This is Buddy Lawson from the Library Board and this is Mrs. Clark," Celine said by way of introduction.

"No need to introduce us, Celine. Joanna and I go way back," she smirked. Joanna ignored the familiarity that was not mutual as she shook Mr. Lawson's hand.

"Hi, Carol," she said. "What are you doing here?"

"Mrs. Clark is on the City Council," Anne said suddenly at her right elbow. "She doesn't want us touching this wall."

"No, I don't," Carol said. "It will deface the library if you cut a big chunk in the wall! What are you all thinking?" Her indignant look was directed at Joanna. Obviously this woman had a beef with her, but for the life of her, Joanna couldn't think why.

"It's not a 'big chunk,' Carol," Joanna said, seemingly the only one in the room who was prepared to defend the project or whatever they were calling this thing. "It's a small hole just to see what's behind that wall."

"Why do you need to do that anyway?" she asked, her indignant frown looking from Joanna to each member of the party standing in front of her. They all looked at one another wondering what to tell her. Anne's on-the-fly explanation came out rather suddenly.

"We are in a book club, Joanna and I, and we came upon a passage about…well…old buildings from about the time this one was built. The passage talked about rooms that were walled up for no good reason, so we started looking around this building to see if there were any of these rooms here."

"Why this building?" Carol squinted. "What would make you think of this particular building?"

"This is where we hold our book club meetings," Anne responded. "The day we were all talking about these walled up rooms we were having our meeting here in the basement."

Joanna knew there was no book club on the books at the moment. She hoped Carol didn't check the facts Anne was making up.

Carol considered the information for a moment and then quickly discounted it.

"Nevertheless, you're not going through this wall. I don't want our library defaced. It's an historic building," she added. "Anyway, there should be plans somewhere that show a room or not. Look at them instead."

Carol grabbed her purse which she had left on one of the tables and began to leave. Before she got to the door, she turned back.

"And if you do, I'll press charges," she said, then blew through the door letting it slam behind her, gently, of course, because this was an historic building.

The group let out a collective breath and stood there a moment. Finally, Mr. Lawson spoke.

"I am truly sorry, ladies," he said. "I never told anyone about this and didn't expect anyone to block our efforts."

"It's not your fault, Buddy," Anne said, patting his arm. "Why would anyone get in the way of progress?"

"Small-minded people, that's who," Joanna said and Celine only nodded. She was terrified of losing her job because of this. Lawson seemed to become aware of her and her situation in an instant.

"Don't worry, Celine," he reassured her. "No one is going to fire you for this. You're just another concerned citizen."

"Yes, one who's hearing things!" Celine responded.

"I don't think that's it at all," Anne said. "I think you have true believers in the metaphysical aspects of our world in front of you right now, true?" she said, looking around at the nodding heads. Even Sal joined in the nodding.

"Okay, but what are we going to do now? I'm still hearing some sort of activity that no contractor or vermin hunter has been able to find," she said.

"I'll work on this," Lawson said. "Don't worry about it. I'll get in touch with Anne once I get past this self-important troublemaker."

"Thank you, Mr. Lawson," Celine said, shaking hands with him.

"No Mr. Lawson, just Buddy, okay?" he said.

"Okay, Buddy," she said. "And now everyone out…for now at least. I have to close up before anyone else wanders in as some have a habit of doing." Celine looked pointedly at Anne who just smiled and shook her head.

As they all dispersed, Anne walked alongside Sal.

"Thank you for helping us out, Sal," she said, walking through the door he held open for her, holding his power saw in his other hand.

"How did you know who I was?" he smirked.

"Just a guess," she said. "Can you come back if we get permission to do this again?"

"Of course," he said. "Joanna will let me know the date and I'll be here."

"Thank you, though I don't know why I'm thanking you other than I feel there may be some historical significance to this closed-off room."

"Maybe, but we'll see what happens," he said as she got to her car. "Nice to meet you," he said and headed to the back where he was parked.

"Thanks, Sal!" Joanna said, Sal sending a wave over his head as he walked away.

"Don't worry," Anne said as she opened her car door. "We'll get permission."

Joanna just nodded but wondered if she really cared as she got into her own car. Why did she even care if they opened that wall? Really, what was it to her?

"The problem is it's interesting," Joanna said later when she was on the phone with Julia.

"The other problem is you can do it even if you don't want to. You can see or hear these people," she said. "You must be feeling something from this room, something drawing you, or you wouldn't be interested."

"That's true," Joanna pondered. "I am drawn to this space for some reason."

"The librarian isn't going to get into trouble, is she?" Julia asked.

"No, the good thing is the library's board member is a believer and says he will assure she won't," she said. "In fact, he reassured her of that before we left."

"Honestly it sounds interesting to me," Julia said. "If you can help, you should. That's what you've always told me, right?"

"Yes, but what if the gossips in the city get word of this? I wouldn't doubt Carol is spreading it around to her friends right now," Joanna lamented. "I haven't been on Facebook tonight because of that."

"Gossips are going to gossip, Mom. I wouldn't worry about it. It won't hurt your book sales or your career in any way, so don't worry about what you can't control."

"Wow," Joanna said. "I'm impressed! Something I said rubbed off on you over the years!"

"More than you know, Mom," Julia laughed. "Have you spoken to Jim this week?"

"No, is everything okay?" Joanna asked reflexively.

"Everything is fine," she said. "Apparently Margie's belly is getting pretty big, that's all."

"She is eight months along. It's going to happen," Joanna said. "I remember driving somewhere for a weekend with your dad when I was carrying Jim. Luckily I brought a few maternity clothing items with me because by the last day, I had popped! I would not have fit in to any of my regular clothing."

"I remember you telling me that. I'm sure Margie doesn't care. They're both just happy to be becoming parents."

"Are you okay with that?" Joanna worried a little about Julia's single status, but she needn't do so.

"I'm fine, Mom," Julia reassured her. "I have to find someone first, or at least that's the way I would like to do things at any rate."

"I get it. You can be the best auntie when this baby comes."

"That suits me fine for now," she said. "Listen, I'm beat, so I'm going to go, but this was all very interesting. Hang tough, Mom!"

"I will, darling daughter," Joanna said. "Sweet dreams."

After talking to Julia, Joanna decided to continue the quest. People like Carol were not going to stop her out of principal alone. In fact, contrary to Carol's small-minded worries about defacing a building, there could be a benefit to the city. What if they found something truly historical in that room? Worse yet, what if there was a sinister reason it was closed? Shouldn't the citizens know about it?

Though not yet, Joanna thought as she grabbed a glass of water and settled onto the couch in the den with a good book. She didn't want more 'Carols' of the world to obstruct the investigation. She hoped Buddy or Anne could get permission to punch a tiny little hold in the wall, just so they could see what was in that space.

Felix jumped up beside her.

"There's a good kitty," Joanna said and opened up her book, in for the night.

"So what do they think is back there?" Andrea asked Sal after they were flopped in front of the TV, show they were about to watch paused.

"They don't know," he said, savoring a spoonful of cookie dough ice cream. "We just found there's a room with no doors anywhere. It goes back into the main library."

"Do they think it was part of the original building?" Everyone knew about the original building. Its architecture stood out from the main building that had been built on the back of it.

"Again, they don't know," he said. "They want to get a hole in the wall so they can see what's back there."

"And you said they are going to try again to get the city's or the library's approval, right?" she said.

"Yes, so we have to wait."

"Interesting," Andrea said. "Now I also wonder what's back there."

"You'll know when I know, Sweetie," Sal grinned and took a bite of ice cream. "Now put something on. I'm running out of juice here!"

"Okay," she said and turning on the play button while Sal finished his ice cream.

CHAPTER 6

Joanna decided to park her car in the lot by the Green that next Saturday and walk up to the library for the paranormal group meeting. As she reached the building on Campbell Avenue, she saw a man looking around the back of the building. He nodded to her, so she nodded back thinking nothing of it. There was a small parking lot in the back and it occurred to her he may have dropped his keys or some other objects he was searching for. This was until she got to the door and saw him peeking around the side of the building. As nonchalantly as possible, he stepped out of his hiding place and started walking down the street when she caught him. She entered the library shaking her head.

When she got to the bottom of the stairs, she ran into Laura coming back from the Ladies Room.

"That's a look," she said when she saw her. "What's going on?"

Joanna had not realized she had 'a look' on her face and shook it off.

"Nothing, really, just a guy hanging out outside the library," she said and when she held the door open for Laura, she was already up the stairs and out the front door. Joanna waved at everyone's puzzled faces and followed Laura out.

"He's not there anymore," Joanna said.

"Where did he go? Did he drive away? Did he try anything?" Laura said, indignant.

"No, he didn't do anything and he walked down that way," Joanna indicated toward the funeral home on the corner of Washington Avenue a block away.

"Well, what exactly happened?" Laura said, holding the door open for Joanna and following her down the stairs once more.

"I walked up Campbell and saw him in the back of the library. He looked as if he was searching for something when he saw that I saw him, but he suddenly peered around the building at me when I got to the front door."

"He'd have to be pretty fast to have gotten there in that time," Laura said. "Maybe we should tell the librarian upstairs."

"No, he wasn't doing anything," Joanna responded. "It was just weird, that's all. He wasn't threatening me."

"Just the same, he was doing something and we should report him," Laura exclaimed. "He could be a stalker."

"What's this about a stalker?" Anne asked, walking in the door just at that moment, the last of the group to arrive.

"It was nothing, Anne, just a guy outside," Joanna said, trying to end the discussion.

"I don't think it was nothing, though," Laura said, plopping into her chair and crossing her arms in front of her.

"Well, we can figure it out later, as long as you are both okay," Anne said. "We have work to do."

"Any more news from the board?" Nick asked.

"Yes, but they are definitely dealing with opposition within the board and now, within City Council."

"Is it Carol?" Joanna asked. "She was a pill when I dealt with her on the PTA some years ago."

"Me, too," Maria commiserated.

"Yes, it's Carol, but she has somehow infiltrated the library's board as well, and Buddy is having a tough time keeping them on our side."

"Can we do anything?" Laura asked. "Maybe talk to them ourselves?"

"Well," Anne began. "That's what I was thinking. While they did give us permission to poke a small hole in the wall in order to see if anything is back there, they don't want it to become a sideshow and the city is worried about damage to the building. I thought, if Joanna was willing, she and I could have a meeting with the library board and the City Council, if they'll talk to us, and see if she can use her celebrity to get them in our corner."

"I'm happy to do that, but appearing in front of a City Council meeting will just draw attention to the entire endeavor, don't you think?"

"Yes, there are people who actually make going to a City Council meeting a night if you know what I mean," Nick said. "It's ridiculous how small a life these people have that a City Council meeting provides them with entertainment rather than, say, going to a movie or reading a book!"

"I don't know about that," Maria interjected. "By going to the meetings, or at least the ones dealing with things that interest you, you find out what's going on in the city rather than reading someone else's point of view in a news."

"You wouldn't have to go before the Council," Anne clarified. "Buddy said he would call a meeting of the Library Board and ask Carol and one or two other members of the council to attend as his guest for an informational session."

"Where would they hold it?" Sylvia asked from her quiet position across from Joanna. She almost had forgotten she was there; she was so quiet and unobtrusive as if she was trying to hide into herself.

"They usually have them in this room," Anne said. "What do you think? I'll go with you," she added, hoping to make Joanna more comfortable with the plan.

"No problem, I'll go," Joanna said.

"Do you want me to call Celine or do you want to do it?" Anne asked.

"I have no problem with you taking a more active role with her," Joanna said. "It will make her more comfortable with you and having this group part of the investigation rather than just me."

"It's funny because I didn't think you were very interested in having anyone outside this group and maybe the police department know you had any of these gifts," Nick chuckled.

"I wasn't, but I feel compelled to help Celine. If Anne calls her, I'm technically less involved, or it seems to me as that's how it will read," Joanna said.

"It may and I'm happy to do it," Anne said. "Now, what do you think we might find in there?"

And the group was off and running with speculations as Anne had intended. She winked at Joanna while the rest of the group had their heads over their phones gathering information about ghosts and their sightings.

Joanna did not want to get involved in using her latent gifts, but she found the 'noises-in-the-library' issue compelling. Since they could only get into the library at night after the library closed, it did not interfere with her real work; the writing projects she had going for herself and a few clients. Plus Joanna couldn't help but be a helper when she was needed. She had always had a difficult time declining requests for help with school functions when the kids were little, especially a book sale. She had been a sucker for the book sales, often quietly purchasing a book for a child or two who came to the sale without any money. Joanna hoped she had created a few serious readers by doing so, but she would never know. Parents of those kids never bothered to find out who got their child a book or even thank them if they did find out. It was, sadly, the way of the world these days.

"There are so many houses and buildings in Connecticut that are haunted," Maria said, flipping through the pages on her phone.

"They're in all states and countries," Nick said. "It's a wonder we don't have more people interested in the paranormal."

"I think they're just afraid of what they don't know," Laura said, glancing up from her phone.

"Well, I'm going to rely on you guys to send me information about this library and this possible haunting, if you find any," Joanna said.

"I have a lot going on and appreciate the help now that I see it in action!"

The group muttered, "No problem," and "Sure," while their faces were firmly glued to their phones. Joanna and Anne smiled at one another and left them to it until the end of the meeting.

CHAPTER 7

"Yes, I can't believe it's already June!" Joanna said into the phone. Her editor was filling her in on the status of the latest book they were publishing. It was due out July first which was just a month away. "Do you have anything scheduled for me other than that mid-July book festival in Redding?"

Joanna was always happy to publicize her books if it meant a few sales, and Redding was a pretty little town. It screamed "Connecticut country!" which seemed to be what all of the city dwellers in New York City looked for in a weekend home. Personally, Joanna didn't understand working all day on Friday and then schlepping two or three hours in a car only to do it all again on Sunday afternoon. She didn't live in the city, that was true, but if she did, she would much rather go to Central Park or down to the Battery if she wanted to be outside, or even take in a museum or have coffee at a sidewalk café somewhere.

"No, that's about it," Lisa responded. Joanna could hear her clicking through her online calendar. "This is a slow summer, but I'm working on a couple of opportunities here and there. You never know what August or even September will bring. Keep me updated on any long vacations, okay?"

"Of course," Joanna said. "Or baby news. Remember my son's baby is due over the summer, so I'll have to stay within an hour or two's drive. I'm here if you need me around that, though."

"I completely understand. I'll keep you updated. Thanks!" Lisa said and hung up.

Joanna always thought it was funny how Lisa ended a phone call. No, " 'Take care," or even " 'Bye!" before she hung up. She just hung up! She had already asked about Margie and her pregnancy, but Joanna felt the need to remind her. Joanna had no problem cancelling if she was needed by her son when the baby was born. Lisa knew that, but it did bear reminding such a busy person.

As soon as that call ended, another one came in. It was Anne.

"Hey there!" Joanna said into the phone.

"Hi," Anne said. Without preamble, she launched into the reason for her call. "I talked to Buddy and we're a go for tomorrow night."

"What does that mean? We can drill that hole?"

"Yes, but we want to do it quickly in case the board changes its mind," Anne said.

"Or Carol and her cronies come back," Joanna said. "I get it. Sal's here today, so I'll ask him if he's free. Assume he is unless you hear otherwise. What time?"

"The library closes at 8:00, so I'd say 8:30 to be safe. I'll see you then."

"Okay," Joanna said. " 'Bye."

Joanna sat there for a moment, listening to the sounds of her contractors in the house. Would Sal agree to go to the library again in order to poke a hole in the wall? She was concerned he would be leery of getting involved again due to the controversy, but she need not have worried. When she went up to the room where he was working and asked him to accompany them again, he did not hesitate.

"Of course I'll be there," he said. "I'm dying to know what's behind that wall."

"Can we come?" Mario asked with Rob looking on expectantly from his place by the back wall.

"No, I don't think so," Sal said.

"Not right now anyway," Joanna seconded. "We'll probably be able to include you guys once we find something."

"Do you think you will?" Rob asked. "What could be back there anyway?"

"Yeah, a room without a door," Mario marveled. "How cool is that?"

"I totally agree," Joanna said. "Okay, Sal. I'm going back to work."

"Us, too," he said to his guys as Joanna walked away.

Joanna couldn't help her curiosity as to what was behind that wall. Why would anyone build a building, or even add on a room, with no door? There had to be something in there. It was also strange that this room did not show up on the blueprints. Perhaps there was another set of blueprints or another version? Joanna tried not to think about it. She put it out of her mind as she went back to work writing.

The next evening was much the same with the same people in attendance. Joanna walked in with Anne who was waiting for her outside with Buddy. The next person was Laura, then Nick who burst into the room just as Sal was marking a small 6" by 6" square on the wall with a square pencil.

"Sorry I'm late," he said to the startled onlookers. "I had a big project to finish." Joanna knew Nick was working freelance for a couple of news organizations and made a mental note to ask about his latest project. They often commiserated on the stuff they wrote to pay the bills, but they kept meaning to meet for coffee but hadn't yet. They were both pretty busy which they both thought of as a good thing.

"Are we ready now?" Sal grinned as he messed with Nick.

"We're good," Nick said. "Let 'er rip, Sal!" The two men knew one another from a job Sal did at a newsroom Nick used to work at.

Sal turned on this electric saw and lightly led its edge along the lines he had marked and cut the square, gingerly so as to avoid whatever was behind those cuts. He cut two sides of the square and then took a razor on a handle and scored the other two sides, top and bottom, before jimmying the square out of its place and leaning it up against the wall at his feet. As it came out, the small crowd collectively leaned forward to see what was behind.

"Wow," Sal said as he peered at the place behind the square of plaster. "I think it's a door," he said, looking closely through the 6" x 6" hole he had just carved out of the wall.

"Some sort of wooden door," Celine added.

"It sure is," Buddy said. "It also looks very old, doesn't it?"

"I would say so with that dark brown coloring and, wait. It looks like old nails or spikes holding the wood together." Sal got in closer, took out his camera and took a few photos.

"That's a good idea, Sal," Joanna said, grabbing her own camera out of her purse. "I'm going to snap a few, too."

"Does anyone know anything about architecture?" Anne asked the room. "Maybe we should get someone in here to find out how old this is."

"I'm not sure I want to add another person to this crew, do you?" Celine asked looking at Buddy.

"I agree, but if we go any farther, I have to go back to the damn board again and that means the City Council folks are going to hear about it," Buddy responded. "I hate to do it, but this is a public building."

"I understand," Celine said. "Maybe we should hide the hole with something, maybe a picture?" she said. She walked around the Reference Room and saw a larger painting of a dog hunting some birds. It lived on the wall behind the book stacks at the back of the adjacent room. No one would notice it missing, so she went over to it calling for Sal to follow her. The two pulled it off the wall and were gratified to see it was only hung with a wired on a heavy nail. Celine would look in the storage room for something else to put in its place when she got to work the next day. The place behind the painting made it obvious there was something missing. For now, she and Sal gently lifted it from its place.

"Do you have another nail heavy enough to hang this, Sal?" Anne asked.

"I do," he said, examining a handful of nails pulled from his tool belt. "These are from your house, Joanna. I figured they might come in handy somehow. I'm glad I didn't empty my tool belt today."

"Me, too," Joanna said, watching Sal gently tap a nail into the wall after he replaced the piece of wall he had just cut out. The picture would lay centered over the hole he had just created. It was also at the perfect height.

"That looks good," Buddy said. "Now, again, we will have to reconvene after I call the board tomorrow."

The group dispersed. When she got home, she toyed with the idea of going into her office to check her email one last time but decided to scan her email on her phone instead. She usually did not check her email at night preferring to leave work during work hours if at all possible, but for some reason her emails were calling to her tonight.

Joanna poured a glass of water, popped some ice into it and got comfy on the couch in the den. While she flipped, she saw the usual emails selling her things, saying, "Thank you," and then selling her things with a promo code, newsletters she didn't want to read, until she came to an email from someone with a library url at the end of their email and a subject line saying he was on the library board. She clicked on it.

Dear Ms. Davis,

I understand you are investigating an area of the West Haven Library building and would like to discuss your involvement. Would you be kind enough to meet me at Elm Diner at 11:00am on Saturday? I would like to buy you a cup of coffee and talk about what a bad idea I think this is.

All The Best,

Ron Adamson

Joanna blinked into her phone. What the heck was this now? She wondered if he was a friend of Carol's of PTA and City Council fame. Either way she was going to go. She had to out of curiosity. Why would another person have a problem with or even notice she was investigating the library? Joanna didn't think anyone had an interest in the library, but she seemed to be completely wrong about this. She only hoped they put as much time into finding books to take out as they did to worrying about whether or not someone touched the walls!

Shaking her head, Joanna put the phone down and looked for something to watch from her DVR list.

CHAPTER 8

"So, yes," Joanna said into the phone. "I got an email from someone named Ron Adamson yesterday."

"Ron emailed you?" Anne said. "What did he want?"

"Do you know him?"

"He's on the library board. Of course I know him. How don't you?" Anne asked astonished. "His name is always in the papers for one thing or another. He's very philanthropic."

"Ah, well, I literary never pick up the local papers. Ever," Joanna said. "Maybe I should, but they don't interest me."

"So what did the email say? What did he want?" Joanna could almost hear Anne jumping up and down in her chair across town.

"He wants to meet me at Elm Diner on Saturday to tell me why investigating the library isn't such a good idea," Joanna responded. "Why do you think that might be?"

"I have no idea. Maybe he's a friend of Carol's?" Anne offered.

"I don't know, but I'm definitely curious."

"You'll have to fill us in at the meeting after," Anne said. She and Joanna chatted for a while before hanging up and getting back to a story about the metaverse and NFT's. She had no idea what it was all about, but the metaverse was touted as being the next big thing like the internet was when it began. Joanna needed to interview one more person before writing her story, so she got to it.

On Saturday, Joanna walked into the diner looking for Mr. Adamson and directed to a booth in the back. He stood up as she approached and reached out his hand.

"Nice to finally meet you, Ms. Davis," he said. "I've enjoyed some of your books."

"Thank you," she said, taking a seat and stowing her purse beside her. The waitress took her order of a coffee and a water, refilled Adamson' cup and left. "To what do I owe the pleasure?"

"Well, I'm not sure you'll think it's a pleasure, but I wanted to have a little chat," he said, taking a sip of his coffee.

"I'm listening," she said, accepting her own cup from the waitress and adding an ice cube from her water glass. It used to drive John crazy when she did that, but she didn't like scalding hot coffee. It burned her tongue. Mr. Adamson looked up from his own cup and began telling Joanna what she expected he would tell her.

"I don't want you continuing this excavation of the library I've heard about," he said.

"Why not? I'm sure you've also heard about what we found behind the wall," she said. "Why wouldn't you want to see why that room was built?"

"Because I don't want to damage the building," he said.

"It will bring life to that building if we find out what's behind that door," Joanna countered. "At the very least, there will be another

Ghostly Passage

room to store things in such as books and papers important to the library…maybe even the city." But Adamson was unmoved.

"I don't think so and I don't want to see that wall destroyed in any way by hacking into it," he said.

"I disagree and I'm going with whatever the library board decides," she said, sipping the coffee she now knew she would be leaving to get cold. Too bad because it was good coffee. As she sipped, an image came into her head.

"Wait, were you the person I saw in the back parking lot of the library a few nights ago?"

"I'm not sure what you're talking about," he said, breaking eye contact with her.

"Yes, it was you," she said. "What were you doing there that night?" He looked a bit shaken.

"I was getting into my car, of course," he said.

"Then why did you walk down the street when I caught sight of you in front of the building? And why did you do so if you had your car?"

Adamson had nothing to say. He just sipped his coffee, finally looking up at her above the rim of the cup.

"Well, we're going to continue if we get the board's approval," she said, taking a five out of her wallet and putting it down on the table. "I hope we meet in better circumstances in the future." She stood and turned back to face him. "I don't believe anyone has any bad intentions about ruining the library, just so you know. The group that's involved just wants to find some answers."

"Answers to what questions?" he said. Joanna hesitated a moment.

"That's classified right now, but we don't want to hurt the building at all," she said. She was about to thank him for the coffee or for meeting her, but she had paid for the coffee and he had requested the meeting, so she stopped there, turned and left with a quick nod.

Joanna mused about what a strange, uninformative meeting that had been. She had learned nothing other than Adamson was on the side of the fence that did not want the library tampered with, but for no good reason she could surmise. They had found a door to a room that was not used, or not that they suspected so far. Wasn't he curious to find out what was in there or why the door was covered over? This was getting stranger and stranger, and Joanna looked forward to filling in the group in a couple of hours.

"Ooh," Sylvia said when Joanna reported back to the paranormal group. "Maybe he knows something."

"Maybe, but did it sound as if he was just worried about the building like Carol says she is?" Nick interjected.

"That's not the feeling I got," Joanna said. "I'm not basing this off anything he said, but it felt as if he was hiding something."

"What could he be hiding, though?" Anne said. "That part of the building was built at the turn of the 20th century and the new part in the early '60's."

"I have no idea, but now I have no reservations about pushing forward to find out what's in there," Joanna said.

"Well that's great because we just got permission to expose that door," Anne said with excitement which got the rest of the group excited. She heard from Buddy right before she left the house and was bursting to tell the paranormal group.

"That IS great!" Joanna said.

"Yes, and Buddy says he can be there any night this week," Anne said. "I think it's best if we have him with us as a representative of the board, don't you?"

"I have no problem with that and I'm sure it reassures Celine," Joanna said. "I'll find out when Sal is available and let you know."

"That sounds perfect," Anne said.

"Do you think Celine will let us come this time?" Maria asked, her eyes wide with anticipation.

"I'll ask," Anne replied. "We'll have to abide by her wishes, but now that she knows about our little group, I don't think she would have any objection. We'll see what she says."

"Thanks, Anne," Maria said. "It just so interesting to me!"

"I agree. Now, let's talk about Sylvia's haunted house for a change. Any news, Sylvia?"

And the group dove into the subject. It was a relief to talk about something other than the library which, Joanna mused, they didn't even know for sure was haunted. The problem was that Joanna thought it was. She got strong vibes from that area of the library and always had. Of course she just wrote it down to the building being old on old land. Anything could be walking around there even residual energies from long ago.

Joanna grinned to herself. She had been watching too many ghost investigation shows! She focused on the subject at hand: Sylvia's haunted house.

Tuesday evening arrived and the group, plus Sylvia and Maria this time, leaned forward en masse and peered over Sal's shoulder where he was about to cut.

"Can you guys step back a little while I do this?" Sal asked. "There's going to be stuff flying and you don't have on safety glasses."

"I'm sorry, Sal," Anne said and stepped back along with the rest of the group.

Sal had already marked four straight lines with his pencil, what he suspected was the outline of the door, and began sawing with a shallow touch on the long lines on each side. When he was finished, he took a razor-type device, similar to a box cutter, and gently scored the top and the bottom lines. As he tugged from the top, the piece gently came off with a puff of dust. He laid the piece of wall to the side and whistled.

"That's an old door," he said. "I bet it was built when the library was first built."

"Those plans were lost in a house fire when they were moved for 'safe keeping' to someone's house during the work for the addition, sadly," Celine said. "They re-wrote the blueprints during the work and never included a door."

"Do we want to open it?" Nick asked. "It's kind of spooky, but I'm dying to know what's behind that door."

"Me, too," Sal said. "That is if it's okay with all of you."

Ghostly Passage

"Yes!" was the resounding response, so Sal put down his saw and reached for the doorknob. He shook it gently to make sure it wasn't going to come off in his hand, then turned it.

The door opened.

The room's contents were disappointing. It had a tamped-down dirt floor and a musty, old odor causing everyone to back even farther away from Sal.

"It looks like a closet," Maria said.

"So why wouldn't they have used it as a closet when they built the rest of the build behind it?" Celine asked the room. "The floor is still dirt rather than any type of flooring."

The smell had an overpowering scent of must, mold and something rotten, though there was nothing in the room that they could see when Sal looked from the doorway with his pen light.

"Well, have a look before I close it again," he said, walking to the side and fanning the stench from his nose.

They all looked into the room while holding their nose and lighting up their phones. There was truly nothing. It was an empty room.

"It's funny," Anne said. "There is no door on the other side where it should be if it had been used as a storeroom."

"That is strange," Joanna said when it was her turn to look in. "Maybe this door led outside when the library was first built?"

"Maybe, but you would think they wouldn't cover over the door unless someone had something to hide," Nick added.

"Maybe we can all do a little research and see if we can figure this out together?" Buddy suggested.

"Should we clean it out?" Sylvia asked.

"No, we shouldn't," Joanna said. "That might disrupt whatever historical value it might have if it has any at all."

"I agree," Maria said. "We should just leave it alone for now. We can figure out if we should do anything with it once we get more information."

"That sounds perfect to me," Buddy said. "The only problem is there's a big hole here now, a hole that has a door. Can you put that piece of wall back up for now? Will it still fit?"

"Yes it will," Sal said, already reaching for the piece he had just cut out. "You can take one of the bookcases and put it in front of it if that's not too heavy."

"No, they are quite heavy and the patrons would notice," Celine said. "I have an idea." She scurried out of the room and returned with a large tapestry. "This was in the storeroom and has a pocket at the top where there's already a rod inserted. If you use these hooks I found, you could probably nail them into the wall and hang the fabric from the rod. What do you think?"

"You should be a decorator!" Maria said. "That looks big enough to cover that door, too."

"You could tell the patrons you were trying out a new way to decorate or use the library's pieces or something," Laura said. "Would they buy it?"

Ghostly Passage

"I think they would," Celine said, handing over the hooks which Sal nailed up after carefully measuring the placement.

When Sal was finished, the group stepped back to admire his work while he re-hung the picture they had just replaced with the tapestry.

"It looks good to me," Buddy said. "What do you think, Celine? Will it get past any nosy patrons?"

"I think it will," she said. "Even if they touch it all they will feel is a wall behind that tapestry."

"Okay, everyone," Anne said. "I think we'll let Celine close up the library. Let's get going."

"And I'll look into the formalities of investigating that room," Buddy said. "I'll contact you when I find out something," he said, nodding at Anne.

"Thanks, Bud," Anne said, patting his arm. "I'm glad I roped you into all of this!"

"Actually, so am I! This is fascinating and I want to know what's up with that room."

"I'll wait to hear from you," she said, following the group from the room with Buddy close behind her and Celine in the back of the line so she could shepherd everyone out of the room and the front door like a field trip of elementary school students.

"Thank you, everyone," she said, turning the key in the lock after Anne and Buddy moved through the door and out of the building. They all looked back and saw her waving through the glass door. They waved back and headed to their car.

"'Bye, everyone," Joanna said to the sound of goodbyes and 'see you laters throughout the parking lot. She got into her car and drove home. When she arrived, she dropped her bag, pet Felix and went into her office to start researching. First, she looked up the library and the era in which it was built to see if there was any mention anywhere of doorless rooms. If she found that, she might find out its purpose. Unfortunately, after an hour of searching, she found nothing. She did, however, find a variety of other tidbits which she had written down on her scratch pad, a necessity she always kept near when she was going down the Google rabbit hole of information. On it was written "underground railroad." It was yet another trail to follow, so she typed it in the search bar.

As she imagined would happen, there was a lot of information from which to choose to search, so she started at the beginning and worked her way through the first three pages before, having had enough, she saved the search, turned off her computer and went to bed with the latest novel she was reading.

"So it was just a closet?" Andrea asked Sal when he got home that night.

"Yeah, all dirty and musty like it had been closed up for a long time," he said, pulling off his work boots at the door and placing them on a mat kept there for that purpose. He headed to the kitchen with Andrea on his tail.

"What are they going to do now? If it's empty, that should be it, right?" she said, going to the sink to get him a glass of cold water before handing it to him and joining him at the kitchen table. He took a long gulp.

"They are going to look into getting permission to look at it more closely," he said. "For now the library found a big rug to put over the hole and I put back the piece of wall I cut out."

"What, a tapestry or something?"

"Yeah, that's it. She called it a tapestry. She found it in a back room somewhere. It fit over the hole perfectly when I hung it up."

"Did it come with a pole or anything? I can't imagine they would let anyone nail a tapestry directly on the wall."

"Yeah, one side of the tapestry had a dowel or some sort of pole through it. I put it up with couple of hooks she found. It's not going to hurt the wall," he added.

"That's good," she said. "I know you know what you're doing, so it's good they asked you to be involved."

"I hope so," he said, taking another gulp of his water. "I have a feeling this might turn out to be something instead of just an empty closet."

"What gives you that idea?" Andrea asked.

"For one thing, it's not a room that should be there. At least that's what they all thought when they talked about it," Sal replied.

"So what's next??"

"I just have to wait and see for now," Sal said, finishing off his water and bringing the glass to the sink. "I don't want to talk about it anymore. I need to do something else for a while before I go to bed or I'll b dreaming about an empty closet all night."

"No problem," she said to his retreating back. She flipped off the kitchen light and followed him into the living room where they flopped on the couch and watched TV.

It wasn't to be the end of Joanna's day, though. At around midnight, just after she fell asleep, she got a call from Jim telling her Margie went into the hospital. It was only the beginning of July, so he was alarmed. Her parents lived in Florida, about thirty miles from Joanna's mother, so Joanna was the person they called if they had a problem. By the time she got to the emergency room a half an hour later, she found Margie sitting up in a bed chatting with Jim.

"Did your water break?" Joanna asked her to which she shook her head.

"No, just strong pains," Margie said. "The doctor wanted me to meet her here because it's still a couple of weeks until the delivery date." Margie was due in late August.

"Well, that is pretty close," Joanna said. "Can I get you anything? A glass of water? Coffee for you, Jim? I'm not even sure there's anything open, but I'm sure I can manage some ice water," she said, peeking out of the curtain surrounding the ER bay and scanning the busy ER.

"We're both fine, Mom," he said, pulling over a chair so she could sit down. Joanna found out they were waiting for the doctor to see if he wanted Margie to be admitted or released home.

"What's going on with the library?" Margie asked, making conversation while they waited.

"Funny you should ask," she began and then told them both about the discovery of the door.

Ghostly Passage

"Maybe it's just a closet?" Jim surmised.

"That's what we thought, but the door makes it look as if it was built as a door leading outside. That part of the library behind it wasn't built at that time, so why did they close it up when they did build it?"

"That sounds like a nothingburger to me," Jim said.

"Jim!" Margie slapped his hand that was holding her hand with her other. "Don't be nasty."

"I'm not being nasty, but if it's a door that led outside and then they just built around it, it sounds as if it's a closet they just didn't use."

"That's what I wondered, but why would they build a closet with a dirt floor? Wouldn't they cover it with linoleum or something?" Joanna asked.

"That sounds intriguing," Margie said. "Did you feel anything when you were there?"

But Joanna didn't have the opportunity to answer because just then the doctor arrived.

"You're fine," she said. "You can go home. Those were just Braxton-Hicks contractions, not real ones. Your body is getting ready to welcome your little one to the world!"

"They were pretty strong for Braxton-Hicks," Margie said, rubbing her big belly.

"They sometimes are, but you're still not having the baby tonight," she smiled. "I know by now you wish you were, though."

"Exactly! I'm as big as a house!" Margie lamented.

"Don't worry. It's all normal even being as big as a house," Dr. Levin reassured her. "You can go home, but make sure you rest more. I'll have the discharge orders brought to you as soon as they're ready. Call me if you have any other concerns," she said and walked out of the curtained area of the ER.

"Thank you!" Margie said, then turned to Jim. "Get me outta here, Sweetie."

"I'm already on it," he said, grabbing her clothing and handing to her.

"I'll wait outside while you get ready," Joanna said, closing the curtain behind her and walking to the nurse's station to wait. She was grateful all was well with her little grandchild. They still didn't know the sex, but Joanna felt it was a girl from the very start and she had not been wrong yet when she predicted the sex of babies her friends carried. She didn't know why, but she could always predict the sex of a baby on the way. Joanna didn't expect this time to be any different.

Jim pulled the curtain back and had Margie holding on to his arm.

"I'm not an invalid, Jim," she said, protesting the extra help.

"I know, but you're not exactly balanced these days," he said, not taking no for an answer.

"I'm not saying anything," Joanna grinned when Maggie looked to her for help. "I'm just the mother-in-law."

As they walked out to the car, Margie asked again about the library and the investigation.

"Oh, they're all in an uproar about the door we found," Joanna replied. "I don't even think I want to be bothered with this anymore. 'Too much drama."

"I think you should continue on," Margie said, maneuvering the curb. Jim had parked in the small lot in front of the children's hospital ER, so she walked directly to the car. "If not you, then who, you know?"

"I know what you mean, but it is tiresome having to get permission for this and dealing with power-hungry people like that Council member, Carol."

"Yeah, but you said that other person, that Board member was helping you get the permissions you need," Jim said, opening the car door and helping Margie into her seat. "Are you good?" he asked her.

"I'm fine," she said, taking her purse while he put the 'Go Bag' in the back seat.

"Okay, kids, I'm leaving," Joanna said. She leaned in to kiss Margie on the cheek and then gave Jim a great big hug after he shut the door. "Make sure you call me if anything happens or you need anything at all, okay?"

"We will, Mom. Don't worry," Jim said, squeezing her arm and walking to his side of the car.

Joanna smiled as she walked away despite the tension of the situation. Babies were born all the time, she reminded herself as she walked back into the building and through the lobby to get to the parking lot on the other side of the hospital where she parked her car. This time of night was no time to go walking outside around the hospital. She was glad they had that parking lot available to emergencies right outside the front door of the hospital so Margie either didn't have to walk too far or didn't have to wait for Jim to get the car.

One of the things her 'gifts' were good for was to 'feel' the outcome of events, but it was usually not accurate when it came to family. Joanna tried to check in to what she called 'the cloud,' borrowing from the Internet world. Briefly, as the door was closed while the elevator traveled to the third floor and the entrance to the parking structure, Joanna tuned in. She got a positive feeling when she visualized Margie, Jim and the baby, as she always did. Joanna was reassured by the time the elevator door opened that all would be well and she continued on to her car.

Joanna could not wait to become a Grandma. She never thought she would feel so, well, typical! Everyone who has a grandchild says how exciting it is, but she figured it would be great, of course, but just not this great. She couldn't wait to babysit so Jim and Margie could have a break when the baby was little and enjoy sleepovers when he or she was old enough to enjoy and remember time with their grandmother. She said a prayer that everything would be okay with the pregnancy and headed home to crash for a few hours before Sal & Company arrived to work on the back room.

CHAPTER 9

Joanna finished her 'real' work by Thursday afternoon and decided to get a jump on the library research. She opened up her browser and clicked on the bookmarks she had made for herself. They were all about the West Haven Library and when it was erected as well as when the addition was built. She read about the abolition of slavery, how people escaped and how that empty closet at the back of the original building might have played into all of it. It was just a hunch, but Joanna's senses were telling her that empty, closed-off room contained at least one lost soul, maybe more. She knew this because as soon as Sal opened that door, it was as if someone rushed at her in a flurry of energy. Joanna had no other way to describe it. When that happened, she got the impression of a very young person, a boy, who had something to say, but Joanna did not listen at that moment. She blocked her sense that would let in someone from the other side. She would deal with all of it, or all of them, when she was ready.

Joanna read on. She read about how enslaved people lived under the worst conditions while servicing their masters' homes, farms and plantations. Some of the masters took pity on their slaves and treated them relatively well, if one could consider enslaving a person in the first place 'treating them well.' These slaves were given enough food, not usually beaten, and were allowed to get married with their family sometimes living together. For a time, some were even given their freedom by their masters. This was not the norm, though. Most slaves were beaten, their families torn apart with children being sold to locations far from their parents, and many made the desperate decision to escape and travel north where slavery did not exist. Even if they got to safety, they could be recaptured and brought back to their owner. Slave Catchers did a brisk business before the Emancipation Proclamation was signed in 1863.

Joanna needed to visit the closet alone so she could 'hear' what the souls were trying to tell her or anyone who would listen. She picked up the phone.

"Hi," Anne said when she answered. "What are you up to?"

"Research," Joanna replied. "I'm learning about the Underground Railroad." Joanna had mentioned her suspicions to Anne, but they had not really spoken about it.

"Hmmm. I figured you were going to follow that trail, but I don't believe there was a room behind that door when the original library was built," Anne reasoned. "Why would you research the Underground Railroad?"

"Because there was a building on that site before the library building," Joanna said and proceeded to fill Anne in on her suspicions. "If there was another house or building there, the area where the door is could have been an entrance to the building or a room like a basement." Joanna paused. "Am I reaching?"

"No, I don't think so," Anne said. "Do you know what building was on that site before?"

"Not yet. I'm going to see if I can find any land records at City Hall tomorrow," Joanna responded. "Do you want to come?"

"Sure! I love researching. It's like a treasure hunt."

"It is! I'll pick you up at 11? We can go to lunch after," Joanna offered.

"That sounds perfect," Anne said. "I'll see you at 11."

The two rang off and Joanna got back to her research. There was a lot to learn.

The next day found Joanna and Anne in the City Clerk's Office. Of course, there was talk around town about the ghost in Joanna's house. The Clerk, Mimi, remembered Joanna's previous visit to dig up the plans for her house and was very helpful. Thank goodness Mimi only asked a question or two about the investigation and gossiped about Tommy's fate a bit before she went to find the files Joanna had requested. Joanna wasn't planning on spending a long time here. Now that they had agreed on lunch, she was hungry for seafood down by the beach.

"My goodness," Anne lamented after Mimi walked away. "Do people have anything to do beside be in your business around here?"

"I'm sure it's everywhere," Joanna suggested. "I mean she probably hears all of the town's gossip here with people always going in and out. At least about who's buying or working on property."

"I suppose," Anne responded. "She's probably just making small talk or trying to make a connection with the famous author."

Joanna laughed. "Would you stop that stuff? No one knows me aside from my ghost fans and the occasional bookworm."

"I don't know. I think you underestimate your star power," Anne giggled.

"Or the power of a good ghost story," Joanna replied just as Mimi returned with a pile of papers and maps.

"Here you go," she said, plopping them on the high counter in front of them "You are welcome to use that table off to the side there," Mimi said offering them a small table pushed against the side wall. It had two chairs but was a tight squeeze as it was also up against the counter on one side.

"We'll do that," Joanna said and carried the pile over to the table. When they sat down and had stowed their purses, Joanna took out a pen and a small pad of paper. She wrote, "Let's not talk a lot. They are listening," and pushed the pad in front of Anne who nodded. It felt all cloak and dagger, but the less people in the town knew right now, the better. Word got around quickly and she didn't want anything else to interrupt her investigation.

The two women researched for a couple of hours with a few stretch breaks in between until Joanna put her pen down and declared, "I'm starved. What about you?"

"I could eat," Anne said. "Can Mimi copy the rest of this for us? There are a couple of documents I want to look through and I'm not sure we'll remember what she dug out with all of this paper."

"Yes, she will," Joanna said. "She did it for me before." Taking a couple of pages from Anne and adding a few she pulled out from the pile, Joanna went back to the counter and called Mimi over. "Would you mind copying these for me? We went through most of the others already, but we haven't seen these yet."

"No problem," Mimi said taking the pile. "I'll be right back."

"Thanks, Mimi," Joanna said and turned to Anne. "So, where are we going for lunch?"

"What about Stowe's? We can get it and sit on the beach across the street," Joanna suggested as Anne nodded with enthusiasm.

"Great idea," she said. "I could use some fried clams."

"I like the strips myself, but maybe some scallops instead," Joanna replied. "And those fries are delicious."

As they chatted about what they were going to eat, Mimi returned.

"Okay, here you go," she said, handing over the pile of copied pages. "Just give me $2 and we'll call it even. I'm not in the mood to count all of those pages."

"Okay," Joanna said, handing over a five. "I appreciate the help."

"No problem. That's what I'm here for. I hope you found what you were looking for," she said, coming around the counter to scoop up the rest of the papers they were not going to take with them.

"Okay, then, I'll see you around."

" 'See you next time!" Mimi said with a smile and headed back behind the counter presumably to return the documents to their proper place in the files.

"Jeez," Anne said when they got outside. "She really must like to file, huh? I hate it."

"Yeah, me too," Joanna said. "She's been there for a few years, so it mustn't be that much of a chore for her."

"She was charming, but I can always feel an undercurrent of gossip when I go in that building," Anne said, pulling open the car door Joanna had just unlocked.

"I agree, but it can't be helped. It's like City Hall is the heartbeat of the town and they all want to know everything that goes on around here," Joanna said.

"You are much nicer than me, I think," Anne grinned. "I'm just glad we got what we needed, or I think we did. I can't wait to look at the rest of this stuff."

"Let's do it at lunch if we can do it without everything blowing away."

"Nah, let's take a break," Anne suggested as Joanna pulled out of the parking lot and headed down Savin Avenue. "We can each take some of the pages and look at them later."

"We don't even need all of this," Joanna said, indicating the pile of papers stuffed into a manila folder she had brought with her. "There was a house on that property that was knocked down about twenty years before. I saw the plans and they line up with that door."

"Did they? I saw you were looking at the plans, but didn't get a good look at them myself," Anne said. "The door lines up with the one we found?"

"It sure does," Joanna grinned. "It looks like the back door from the kitchen that led outside. I took a picture with my phone. Take a look.." She handed Anne her phone and Anne was excited.

"Maybe it was used as a way to get into the house without people knowing," Anne said.

Ghostly Passage

"I think it was, but I have to sit in there by myself at some point. Maybe I can get more information from whoever is haunting that room," Joanna said and turned into Stowe's parking lot.

"You do realize how crazy you sound, right?" Anne grinned. "I know it's all true, but if anyone were to record you in secret…"

"Then don't do that," Joanna grinned back and got out of the car. Their lunch was fried clams for Anne and clam strips for Joanna with fries and an iced tea for both of them.

"I don't know why I don't do this more often," Joanna said, wiping crumbs from her lap. They had decided to sit on the beach and brave the sea gulls after all. They watched them pop out of the sky to land near them and their fries as if they were being inconspicuous and would never be noticed by the women.

"Because you would have a heart attack from all the fried food and gain 800 pounds in the process!" Anne joked, tossing a small French fry to one of the more persistent birds. "So, do you want me to call Celine or do you want to do it?"

"I'll shoot her an email when I get home," Joanna responded. "I'll ask her if I can get in there tonight after the library closes. Maybe no one will find out and I can sit and listen in peace."

"I won't tell anyone, but tell Celine to keep it to herself, too," Anne said. "I'll run interference if anyone else does show up so you can have some peace and quiet."

"Thanks, Anne," Joanna said. They chatted for a few minutes more and then got on with their respective days after Joanna dropped Anne off back at her house.

Joanna was in luck and Celine agreed to have her visit the library after closing that night.

"I appreciate this, Celine," Joanna said as Celine locked the door behind her. "Sal's ready if we need him to open the wall for us," she said, but Celine was already shaking her head.

"I called him ahead of time after you gave me his number and he's already there," she said. "I didn't want a lot of people to be involved, but I figured Sal needed to be the one to open the wall carefully without causing a lot of damage. Anne is here, too."

"Great!" She commended Celine on her quick thinking and then greeted Sal.

"Long time no see!" Sal said over his shoulder as he laid the piece of wall next to the tapestry which he had already taken down. "I just have to open this door and we're ready to go."

"Perfect," Joanna said, dropping her purse and walking over to Sal.

"What do you want to do after I open the door?" Sal asked. "Are you going in there to look around?"

"Yes," she responded. "I just want to sit quietly and see what I can feel, if that makes sense."

"Oh, it makes sense to me," Sal said, turning the handle and pulling the door open. The scent that wafted out of the space was old and musty. "Do you want to use one of my masks I use for dusty jobs? I have one here," he said, pulling one out of his toolbox.

"Thanks, I'd appreciate it," Joanna said and placed it on her face before walking into the void, because that's truly what it felt like.

Ghostly Passage

A void. The unknown. "If you all could just step back so I can be alone, it would be helpful."

Celine and Sal stepped back almost to the entrance of the Reference Room where Anne stood while Joanna walked through the door to the empty closet. It was pitch black except for the entrance where the door was located. The musty smell was probably from years of the space being closed and blocked off to entries.

Joanna reached up to touch the wall. It was cold as expected. As she walked forward with her phone light clicked on, she discovered the room went the length of the main library building. How no one noticed this, she didn't know, but supposed anyone looking at this part of the building would think the wall to this room was part of the main library room which it was, sort of, but not open to anything before the door was discovered. She ran her hand against the smooth wall all the way to the end of the room on the left side. There was nothing in front of her but a solid blank wall much like the one on her left. She turned and laid her hand on the other wall, doing the same and running her hand along it about shoulder height. When she got to the end near the entrance, she stopped. What was that bumpy section on the floor about two feet from the entrance? She flashed the light from her phone on the space but saw nothing unusual. She prodded the floor with the toe of her shoe. She didn't find anything unusual. It just felt a bit bumpy. She ran her hand down to the floor and then up to the ceiling and still nothing felt unusual.

Hmmm, she thought. Joanna would have to get more light in there to see better what was going on. For now, she laid a towel she had been carrying down on the cold, hard floor and sat quietly facing away from the door and closed her eyes. Joanna found closing her eyes blocked much of the external noise and internal clutter in her head, especially when it was dark. It was almost like meditating, but with the expectation of hearing or seeing things or even feeling things that were not there in the living world. She knew it didn't make sense to those who could not live it, but hearing, seeing and sometimes feeling things that were not there was part of Joanna's real world.

As she sat, she immediately felt the presence of a young boy. She didn't hear words but saw an outline in her mind's eye and felt he was trying to tell her something important. She often got what those from the other side were trying to convey by feelings or murky images, though sometimes with clear images like when she met the ghost of Sophia in her kitchen. Joanna often thought it must be a learning curve on the other side just like in the living world. Perhaps it takes some skill or practice to be able to communicate, she mused.

The boy was saying, "Mama." Joanna got the impression he was looking for her and could not find her. She thought that strange since she assumed, based on nothing, that spirits could easily find one another on the other side. She shook her head and waited. A series of images suddenly came out of the mist. The boy's mother was running from something, or at least that's the feeling she got. She was running or escaping from something, fear evident. Could she not get tom him? She asked the boy in that other part of her brain. His response was a resounding, "No!"

Joanna was shaken a bit by the abrupt way her answered, like he was shouting, and briefly opened her eyes. She took a breath and closed them once again, but she could not feel or hear anything more from the young boy. She felt there were other souls in the room, but they did not want to come forward, so she waited a moment. Another moment. Just one more moment, and then opened her eyes, stood up and gathered the towel she had laid down.

When she came out of the closet, the three onlookers stopped their conversation in mid-sentence.

" 'Talking about the crazy author, huh?" Joanna joked as she walked up to them.

"No, not at all!" Celine said. "We were wondering what you saw or heard in there. Speculating."

"Did you see anything?" Anne asked, excitement evident in her inflection.

"Not much, but a little something," Joanna said. "I don't want to say until I've figured it all out which, for me, means writing it all down."

"Okay, so you're done for now?" Sal said, closing the door and preparing to cover it with the square of wall and the tapestry.

"I'm done for now," Joanna said, always surprised at how fatigued this type of work made her. It was as if it sapped her energy a bit. She needed to get home so she could write it all down and crash for the night.

"I need to get back in there by myself again," Joanna told the paranormal group the next day.

"I'm sure Celine would let you go whenever you want, or whenever she was able," Anne said.

"And you're sure we can't come?" Laura asked while Nick nodded furiously.

"No, it's best if I go alone for now," Joanna responded while the group groaned or shifted in their seat. They wanted to help and felt themselves more informed than the average person due to their interest on paranormal concerns, but Joanna did not need help sitting in the room in the dark.

"Can we help with research?" Nick asked. "You know we're good at that. You can tell us what you have already and what you think you need and we can go to town."

"That would definitely help me," Joanna said and told them all about her suspicions about the room somehow being part of a depot for the Underground Railroad.

"How would that be possible if the library was built after the emancipation?" Maria asked.

"I think it was in the house that must have been on the site before the library," Joanna said. "Anne and I think the door we found may have been the back door or a side door to the kitchen."

Joanna spent the next fifteen minutes data dumping the information she had so far to the group while Anne went to find Celine and ask when they could get into the room again. Joanna avoided telling them about her meeting with Adamson, though. She didn't want to stir up any gossip or any suspicions, but Joanna definitely had some.

Anne came back into the meeting room.

"Okay, she said the next good time is Tuesday night," Anne said of her brief chat with Celine. "Oh, wait," she added looking at the group, many of whom were writing down the day and time. "You guys cannot be there, remember?" she said.

"We know," Sylvia said. "We'll behave and not barge in like before."

"We're going to help with the research," Nick added. "I just want to keep track of the dates Joanna goes in there."

"Okay, thanks everyone," she said. "I appreciate your understanding and also your help with the research."

"It's interesting," Maria said. "I mean that's why we come here, isn't it? To learn about paranormal activity and now we have it right in our backyard ... again."

They all chuckled.

"Okay, folks, that's two hours," Anne said and started rising from her chair. "Thank you, Nick," she said when he folded her chair and put it with the others on the chair rack in the corner.

"Good luck, Joanna," Laura said.

"Yes, good luck," Nick said, grabbing his bag.

"Don't worry, we won't barge in," Sylvia said. "Have a good weekend."

"You, too, and thanks again," Joanna said while she walked out with them.

"That's actually going to be helpful," Anne said, turning off the light and heading up the stairs with the group.

"What is?" Joanna said.

"Having the group help with the research," she replied. "They may think of something you or I had not thought about."

"That's true. I welcome their help with this because, even though it doesn't seem so, I have a life beyond this library investigation."

"I know and I'm sure Celine appreciates our help with this issue," Anne said.

"She seems to," Joanna said, reaching her car. She opened the door and tossed her purse on the passenger seat. "Well, I'll see you Tuesday."

"You will?" Anne said, her hand stopping on the handle of her own car door. "I thought you didn't want the group coming with you."

"I don't, but you can help if Buddy shows up," Joanna replied. "I hope he doesn't, but I can't be sure of that if Celine feels she has to let him know what we're doing."

"True," Anne agreed. "Okay, I'll see you then."

Joanna got in her car and pulled out of the parking lot. On the way home, she kept getting flashes of events that seemed as if they fit with the boy in the closet. She had already gotten the image that his mom had to escape something or someone, but how did the boy get here? Joanna would just have to wait until Tuesday night to get more information.

CHAPTER 10

Monday morning arrived with Sal and his workmen. The room was taking longer than Joanna had expected with one little problem turning into a much bigger problem, or just a different problem, as they went forward.

Today it was, "You've got mold in the wall."

"How does that happen? Was there a leak I didn't know about?" Joanna asked Sal, the bearer of bad news.

"It's an old house," he said. "I can show you where the problem is if you want." Sal seemed a little miffed as if Joanna was questioning his integrity.

"No, Sal," she pacified him. "I trust you, of course! I just wish this house would finish giving up its problems to you every time you start working on something."

"Well, we can just close it all up if you really want me to, but that's not going to solve the problem," he suggested. "It will just close up the wetness and the mold in there…"

"Which will create an even bigger problem down the road," Joanna interrupted. "I get it. Do what you have to do."

"Okay," Sal said. He went up the stairs to the spare room and she went to her office, her coffee, thankfully, already in hand. She would need it. Monday was certainly living up to its name.

"Hey, there, Lazy Butt," Joanna said, gently moving Felix from her office chair. "You have an entire couch to lay on, so get off my chair."

The cat purred, stretched and reluctantly fell to the floor with Joanna's gentle nudge.

"Such a drama queen," she smiled.

Joanna made a futile attempt to brush off the cat and hair and then finally gave up. She got off what she could, but she was sure she walked around with Felix's fur on her whether she tried to clean it up or not. She took a sip of coffee while the computer woke up. Punching in her security code, she opened the document and continued her research on nutritional supplements for pets.

"I live such an interesting life, don't I Felix?" she murmured to the sleeping cat and then got on with her day.

In the late afternoon, the crew was leaving for the day and Joanna was saying goodbye when her phone rang. She had left it on her desk, so Joanna had to run for it. She recognized the ring as Julia's or she would have let it go.

"Hi, Sweetie!" she said when she picked it up.

"Hey, Mom," she replied. "I didn't interrupt you, did I?"

"No, I was just seeing Sal and crew off for the day," Joanna said and sat on the couch petting Felix. "What's up? 'Everything okay?"

"Yes, I'm good," Julia said. "I just wanted to tell you about some information I found on the Underground Railroad."

"Does this have to do with the library?"

Ghostly Passage

"Yes," she answered. "I think you were on to something when you mentioned the old house may have been a depot. There were a lot of depots or safe houses around New Haven before Emancipation."

"I know. I just have to figure out what that has to do with this disturbance," Joanna said.

"I think you're right in thinking the house that was on the site before may have been a depot, but they're not depot like you would think of a train depot," Julia informed Joanna. "They're just called depots because it was a place to stop."

"I found that info, too, but I'm just trying to get the logistics straight in my head."

"Well, I bet people came to the back door when they saw the sign it was safe," Julia said.

"Right, like putting a white handkerchief on the clothesline, then they would wait until night and knock on the back door," Joanna responded. "They were really taking a chance, weren't they?"

"Yes, but they were desperate, right?" Julia said. "I can't even imagine."

"Yeah, but who's this boy that I keep feeling?" Joanna said. "He seems young. Do you think a little boy would travel alone?"

"Maybe he was with someone, but they haven't come out to talk yet," Julia giggled. "It's funny how since Sophia, we talk about this ghosty stuff as if it's something everyone experiences."

"I know," Joanna grinned. "That's my life these days."

"Do you want to do it? I mean, I know you're part of that paranormal group, but that was just to get information when you had that ghost in your house," Julia said. "Do you want to help that librarian?"

"I do," Joanna responded. "It's interesting and she needs help."

"Okay," Julia said. "Well, I'm getting ready to wrap up my day here, so I'm going to hang up."

"Okay, Honey," Joanna said. "Keep me updated on anything you find out about the Underground Railroad or any other ideas you have."

"I will, Mom," Julia responded. "I'll talk to you later."

Joanna saw Sal waiting in his truck in the library's parking lot when she drove up on Tuesday night. She pulled in next to him, grabbed her beach blanket out of her trunk and went over to chat.

"Hey, Sal," she said, walking up to his open window. "Thanks so much for coming to help again."

"No, problem," he said. "My wife thinks we're all crazy, but what else is new?"

Joanna chuckled. "Yeah, I can understand that. I can barely believe I'm doing this."

"Don't get me wrong," he said. "She is a total believer, I think, but she thinks it's a lot of trouble for a case of squirrels on the roof or mice in the wall."

"They checked all of that, though," she responded. "I thought the same thing at first, but there is definitely something going on."

"Can you feel something?"

"I can," Joanna responded. "That's why I need to get in there today, to just sit quietly again for a little while and listen."

"And I assume you just want to make sure the wall is safe and the door doesn't break, right? Is that why I'm here?"

"Exactly, but we can get someone else if it's too much of a time commitment for you or too spur-of-the-moment," Joanna prodded. "I don't mind. We're just trying to keep a limit on the number of people who know and might gossip."

"No, no, no! I don't have any problem being here whenever you need me," he hurried. "Don't get me wrong, I'm just asking. I'm a detail guy. I like to know what's going on, that's all."

"Okay, Sal, but please let me know if we're imposing on your time or anything, okay?"

"Absolutely," he said. They stood around for a few minutes until Joanna saw it was 8:25.

"It's time," she said, stepping out of the way so Sal could get out of his truck. "Let's go in."

"I'm right behind you," he said, walking up to the front door of the library. Celine was waiting inside and unlocked the door for them just as Anne walked up from the other direction.

" 'Sorry, everyone," she said. "I parked on Campbell Avenue so it didn't look as if too many people were coming into the library, like an event or something that might draw attention."

"I appreciate that," Celine said. "I hope you're the only other extra guest, though." Celine couldn't help but give Anne the 'Mom look' when she said that.

"No worries," Anne replied. "I'm the only extra person. I came in case Buddy or anyone else showed up. Joanna needs silence and few distractions while she's in there."

"I appreciate that, Anne," she said. The little group walked up the stairs and headed to the Reference Room. Opening the door, Celine asked, "What do you want to do tonight? I never asked Anne."

"Sal, you can get started," Joanna said, nodding to Sal before answering Celine. "I'm just following my instincts here, but I want to sit in the room by myself and see if I can get any impressions."

"Do you mean see something or feel something? What's that mean exactly," Celine said, with an eye on Sal while he moved the tapestry and opened the door.

"I mean whatever happens. It could be seeing something like a shadow or a dark mass, or it could be hearing a voice," Joanna explained. "I may even have a feeling the person had or someone from the other side might touch my arm or something."

"Have you ever had that happen? Someone touching you?" Celine asked, her eyes wide with fear.

"No, no one has ever touched me, but I have heard, seen and gotten the feelings of the person," Joanna said. "Don't look so scared! Nothing is going to hurt you ... or me for that matter."

"It's just so foreign to me," Celine said. "I'm not sure I could handle it if I heard or saw something. Forget if I ever felt something!"

"Don't worry, Celine," Joanna smiled. "Sal and Anne will protect you."

Sal looked surprised at the mention of is name.

"I'm going to run if anything touched me," he joked. "That's something you can count on, so don't count on me to protect you. Talk to Anne here."

"I've got you, Celine," she smiled. "And I don't blame you one bit." Anne tried to explain how things worked to Celine, or at list the way she perceived things worked from her own research and from what Joanna had told her.

"I'm going in," Joanna said as she made her way over to the open doorway. She walked about halfway into the long, empty and dark space, then placed her folded blanket on the floor. With her back to the open door, she sat, ready to take in whatever came at her because she really did not know what would happen.

Joanna settled her thoughts as if she were meditating. She made her thoughts a white noise buzzing blandly in her head. It helped that the spectators in the outer room were keeping quiet enough that Joanna could not hear their whispered conversation. As she sat, the small space took on a slight chill. She waited. Suddenly she got a waft of feelings. That was the only way to put it. The feelings of a young boy slowly drifted to her in the dark.

He was young, maybe three at the most. The image in Joanna's mind was of a short boy, brown-skinned with jet black hair. He was confused as if he was searching for someone. His mother. There were other people around. Joanna called them 'souls' for want of a better word. But those others were not coming forward. Only this one boy wanted to 'talk.'

So Joanna listened.

She got the feeling his mother left him. No, not left him, but passed him off to another adult. Joanna asked if that was correct using that other sense she had. It almost felt like Joanna was dreaming, but not. He immediately said, "Yes!" She tried to listen closer. The next feeling she got was that his mother had been in danger, that's why she passed him off on their trek north, but that could have been Joanna's active imagination. She realized it was not when as soon as she thought it, the boy confirmed she had guessed correctly. She had not really guessed, though, she took in the feeling full of information.

On Joanna sat…on the blanket…alone in the empty room. Except it was not empty in the least. It was full of souls and one boy full of information. Sal, Anne and Celine were there still waiting quietly when Joanna emerged from the dark an hour later and pulled the door closed behind her.

"Did you get any impressions?" Anne asked, the others looking as eager as Anne.

"I sure did, but I have to process it before I tell you all," she said, folding her blanket and grabbing her purse. Joanna had to write it all down with as much detail as possible before she explained it to anyone.

"That's fine with me," Celine said. "It's all kind of spooky to me anyway. I'm not sure I want to hear what you found."

"You can tell me when I'm working at your house," Sal said, already replacing the tapestry.

"You look drained," Anne said, walking next to Joanna as they all left the Reference Room, Celine turning off lights behind them. "Does it take a lot out of you? I never asked before."

Ghostly Passage

"Yes, it kind of drains my energy," Joanna said, passing through the library's front door. Celine closed and locked it behind her as she left with them this time.

"As I've said before, Joanna, I really appreciate your help on this…uh…problem," Celine said. The group looked at her for a moment and then laughed as one voice.

"You can call it that!" Sal said. "Joanna, I'll see you tomorrow bright and early."

"Just let yourself in if I'm not up yet, but I should be."

Sal had finally allowed Joanna to give him a key to her house after all the hours he spent working there on various renovations. At first, he was reluctant to take it saying he didn't want the responsibility and would rather she let him in, but she finally convinced him it was easier for her, especially if she was out already for some reason.

"Yeah," he responded. "You know that's not going to happen. I'll knock or ring the bell when I get there."

"Whatever," Joanna said, and smiled. "I'll see you tomorrow. If you get there around 9, I'll be up already."

"Will do," he said. Sal got into his truck after he tossed in his tool belt and started the engine of his truck. " 'See you!" he said to all before pulling out of the parking lot.

"Thanks again," Celine said, starting her care with Anne doing the same. They both waved at Joanna as they pulled out in front of her.

Joanna sat in her car for a moment. She had to settle the swirl of images and feelings that were going through her brain and body, so she sat there and looked at the brick wall in front of her. So much information passed to her from this little boy that she had to get it down in her notebook as soon as she got home.

She put the car in gear and left the parking lot.

After letting herself into the house, she dropped her bag and went into her office in search of a functional forest green notebook she had. Joanna loved notebooks and always collected them when they were offered at conferences, but this one she had purchased on Amazon. She just couldn't resist it, an A5 size she remembered. She grabbed it off her desk and got comfy on the couch so she could write down all she felt and heard from her night in the empty closet.

Joanna wrote for a few hours and forced herself not to go to the computer to confirm her information. She decided to do it tomorrow. Closing the notebook with the pen marking her place, she placed it on the desk, turned off the light and went to bed.

Detective Sosa was a friend of Joanna's. After the ghost in her house helped solve her own murder, he was a firm believer in the afterlife and Joanna's ability to connect with it.

"Hey, Sosa," Detective Roberts called. "I hear Ms. Davis is investigating again," he said. "Does the city now have a haunted library?"

"I told you, Roberts, don't mess with that," Detective Christopher said. "You saw what happened with that last case. You never know if that stuff is real or not."

"I agree with Christopher," Detective Sosa said. "She gave us information that caught the real killer last time, didn't she?"

Ghostly Passage

"Yeah, I'm just joking with you, Sosa," Detective Roberts said. "I wonder what the problem is this time. Another killer maybe? Squirrels?"

The three detectives chuckled.

"I asked her to help us investigate some cold cases, but just if we need her," Detective Sosa informed the. "She said yes, but we haven't used her services yet."

"Actually, that might be interesting," Detective Christopher said. "We should dig through the cold cases when we have some down time."

"Down time, huh?" Detective Roberts grinned, sorting through the papers on his desk. "If you ever find some down time, let me know and I'll pass some of this paperwork over to you."

"We'll see what happens," Detective Sosa said. "For now I guess she's busy with the library, so we have some time."

"I'm game if you guys are," Detective Christopher said. "What about you, Benny?"

Detective Benny Hines walked in and caught the end of the conversation.

"Sure, I'm in," he said. "What am I in on?"

"We want to use Joanna Davis on some cold cases in the future," Detective Roberts said. "I'm skeptical, but you can't deny she helped us last time."

"Oh, I definitely think that's a good idea," Detective Hines responded. "She helped us last time. And by the way, it took guts for her to come in here in the first place."

"Yeah, we could have all thought she was hallucinating or something," Detective Sosa said.

"You kind of did at first, if I remember correctly," Detective Hines said. "But you were very polite about it."

"And I was proven wrong, wasn't I?" Detective Sosa said. ""We'll see what happens."

All three detectives nodded in agreement as they continued their work, ruminating quietly about the existence of ghosts and their part in the role of police work. Each considered it was worth trying if they ever needed Joanna's otherworldly assistance.

CHAPTER 11

"So, the boy told you his mother gave him to someone else so she could escape?" Nick said.

"Yes," Joanna answered having filled them in on the most recent information she had gotten from the boy in the empty room. The fact that his mother passed him to another adult for the journey, the fact that he did not know where she was, the feeling she got that his mother had been in danger, but they all were, weren't they, Joanna thought?

"His mother could have felt he had a better chance of going with someone else because she was in danger," Laura surmised. "Maybe she was being chased and was able to pass him off."

"That sounds plausible," Joanna said, writing that bit of information down to ask the boy next time she got in the room.

"I read about runaway slaves doing that so at least their children had a chance," Sylvia said. "I started researching after the email you sent us this week. She could have known she was in danger. Maybe someone got wind of her plans to escape and told the master."

"That does sounds possible," Anne added. "I've read those stories, too."

"But wouldn't you think the mother would show up to talk to you, too? To be there with her son?" Maria asked. "I always thought people who had passed could easily find one another."

"Maybe she is there and I just haven't heard from her yet," Joanna said. "There are others there, they are just not talking to me."

"There are?" Sylvia said. "That's fascinating. Can you tell us more about them?"

So Joanna closed her eyes and described the folks she had encountered.

"The boy had on short pants; they were tattered. He had a long-sleeved shirt on, but it looked as if it was made of coarse fabric. No buttons. He came up to my knees or a little past, but not much taller than that. The women had thin dresses that went down to their ankles, some were a bit shorter like the size of a child, but they were adults. There were only a few men, maybe three in total and they all wore pants with simple shirts like the boy. Several of the women had big cloths tied around their heads, and some, men and women, had cloth around their feet instead of shoes. The boy had shoes, but they were too big for him. He was the only child in the group from what I could tell."

"Did they have anything with them?" Anne asked.

"Some had parcels with them, like rags or maybe clothing tied up," Joanna said, as if she was describing a scene before her eyes. "The little boy carried a parcel that looked rather large for him to carry."

"Maybe they all helped one another as they moved around," Nick said.

"It was unnerving being in there, I have to say," Joanna added, opening her eyes. "Even so, I'd like to get in there again to see what I can find out, if I can get more information."

Ghostly Passage

"I'm sure Celine wouldn't have a problem with that," Anne said. "I'll ask before we leave today."

The group tossed around theories for the rest of their meeting before breaking for the day.

"I don't suppose we can come with you, can we?" Nick asked.

"Well, there wouldn't be a need right now," Joanna answered. "I'll just be sitting in a dark room all by myself, for now anyway. I need to see what else the souls want to say."

"Okay," Nick said, standing and folding his chair. "Let me know what else you need, though."

" 'Same here," Laura said doing the same. "This is fun."

"I agree," Sylvia said.

"Me, too," added Maria.

They all got busy putting away the chairs with Nick taking Anne's from her as he usually did.

"I'll see you all next week," Anne said, staying back with Joanna while the others left the basement meeting room.

"Do you want to see if you can get in there sooner or later? I'll go find Celine now," Anne said.

"Sooner would be great," Joanna said. "I feel as if this boy is eager to give me information and I want to take advantage of that."

"Do you have to check with Sal?" Anne said.

"No, he told me he's not going anywhere this summer," she responded. "He just wants a day or two advanced notice if it is possible."

"Okay, I'll go talk to her now," Anne said. "Have a good week!" she said with a wave when they parted at the front door.

Joanna walked up the stairs to the front door and then doubled back. She wondered if she could 'hear' or 'feel' anything if she stood outside the door without moving the tapestry aside. She walked through the doorway of the Reference Room and saw Celine behind the big counter on the right talking to Anne, but she had a concerned look on her face. While Joanna walked toward her to find out what the problem was, Celine nodded her head toward the back of the room. There she saw all the members of the paranormal group milling around the area near the tapestry. There was an old man sitting at one of the nearby tables with the newspaper spread out before him. He was not paying the slightest attention to the group.

This was definitely breaking Celine's rules. If the man got curious as to why the empty Reference Room was suddenly populated with people who were usually not there when he was, he might get suspicious. Who knew which camp he was in, the curious or the argumentative group who did not want the wall touched?

Nick was standing at the end of one of the bookcases and had the class to look sheepish when he saw her. He mumbled something to Laura who was behind him also pretending to look at the books on the shelf. She, too, looked over at Joanna and they both walked over to her. By the time they reached her and Joanna made a motion to follow her out into the hallway, Maria and Sylvia took notice and followed the group. Anne stood by Celine's desk and gave them all the 'Mom look.'" She finished with Celine and then joined the group in the hallway.

"While I welcome your input and definitely your research help, I asked you all to stay away from the site for now," Joanna said, steaming.

"I'm sorry, Joanna," Laura said.

"Me, too," Sylvia and Nick muttered.

"I won't speak for the others, but I was just near there to see if I felt or heard anything," Maria said.

"I understand, but there are those in this city who don't want me to investigate," Joanna responded. "I would rather not give them ammunition. That gentleman reading the paper could be one of those people. We just don't know who is on which side. The less noticeable we are with this investigation, the better."

"We got it," Nick said. "We'll get out of your way."

The group began shuffling to the front door.

"Why were you going in?" Laura asked.

"I was going to clear something with Celine," Joanna said. "Finalize our next meeting *after* library hours," she emphasized.

"I get it," Laura said. " 'Sorry we got in the way."

"You're not in the way," Joanna said. "I appreciate your interest. Maybe Celine will let you all come next time we investigate."

That brightened up the group and made Anne smile and nod to Joanna in agreement.

"I'll see what I can do, but for now, take off, please," Joanna said.

"Yes, Mom," Nick smirked. The group left happy and seemed to be appeased.

Anne turned to Joanna. "Celine said any time this week is good for her. What's best for you and Sal?"

"He may still be at my house, so let me go home and ask him. I'll text you and Celine as soon as I know," Joanna said. "I still have the text string between the three of us."

"Okay, I'll talk to you later," Anne said, both leaving the library.

When Joanna got home she did indeed find Sal. He and the guys were just wrapping up for the day.

"Oh, good," Joanna said. "I'm glad I caught you."

"Is everything all right?" he said, concern masking his face.

"Everything is good with the house, but we need you at the library again," Joanna said. "Is that still okay with Andrea?"

"Oh, she's fine about it," Sal said putting down the tools he was carrying and taking out his phone. "What day were you thinking?"

"Any night that's good for you," Joanna said. "We have to get there, as you know, at 8:15 after the library closes and I would like to get in there earlier rather than later in the week, but only if that works for you. We need you for insurance's sake, you know, making sure we don't mark up the walls, etc."

"I'll text her now and find out if we've got anything going, but I doubt that," Sal said.

He took a moment to text his wife while Joanna went into the kitchen to dump her purse, greet Mario and Rob outside and grab a glass of cold water. By the time she was refilling her glass, Sal came into the kitchen.

"I'm good for any night, too," he said. "How about Monday?"

"I'll text Celine, but I think that would be fine for her," Joanna said, turning off the faucet. "If it's not, I'll let you know, but let's say it's a go for now, okay?"

"Okay," Sal said heading out the back door with his toolbox. "I'll see you here on Monday morning."

"That sounds good, Sal," she responded. "Have a good Sunday!"

"The same to you!" and he was out, packing up the truck and driving away.

Joanna texted Celine and Anne, and all was a go for Monday night.

"Do you want anything, either of you?" Joanna asked, peeking her head out of the kitchen where she had just finished filling the dishwasher for Jim and Maggie. Maggie was having mild contractions again and the obstetrician had told her she was officially on bed rest. The bed at the moment was the couch in front of the TV with Jim parked beside her. Joanna had brought over macaroni and meatballs with, of course, homemade sauce. It was one of Maggie's many cravings during this pregnancy.

"No, I'm good, Joanna," Maggie said.

"Me, too, Mom," Jim said. "Thanks for doing the dishes."

"No problem," Joanna said. She sat in the loveseat and put her feet underneath her. "I want to feel useful. With that said, when the baby comes, feel free to kick me out if you don't want the intrusion. I'm fine with that."

"I appreciate that," Maggie said.

"Do you want to find a movie?" Jim said, reaching for the remote.

"Sure," Maggie said and Joanna nodded.

Jim surfed the movie offerings for a bit before settling on an old movie from the 1940's. The three settled in for a cozy afternoon in front of the TV, Jim and Joanna keeping a close eye on Maggie.

Monday night found the usual group standing around the open door while Joanna sat inside taking in the information. She closed her eyes and worked to silence her thoughts so she could hear what the souls in the room wanted to tell her.

There was the boy again, right up front and ready to talk. Joanna waited at first rather than convey any sort of question. She wanted to see what he wanted to tell her first.

Her first impression from him was that he had travelled a great distance, but maybe that distance seemed great because he was a little boy. He was with someone he didn't know, as he said before, and again, he wondered where his mom was.

Joanna could usually tell when someone had passed. It was as if they stood back in the distance or their image in her mind's eye was murky. This was the impression she got regarding this boy's mother, of course. She also felt she never made it up here to be with him.

"Did your mother pass you off to someone during your journey?" Joanna asked in that other sense and immediately got an affirmative

Ghostly Passage

answer. Like Sylvia had suggested, the boy told her she had handed him over to another adult to take with them while she stayed behind. His dad had been in trouble and his mother told him she couldn't leave him, but she wanted the boy to be safe. She suddenly passed him off to someone and said she would be there soon, but she never came.

She listened for a name, the boy's name. As she waited, a name came to her like a whisper.

"Harry."

Joanna asked in that other place in her senses if this was his name.

"Yes," was the feeling she got, but there seemed to be something else behind that name. It was the best way to explain it. Another name began with an 'J.' She opened the notebook she had brought in with her and wrote that down, then continued to listen to see if she could get anything else on that.

Nothing about the 'S,' but she did get another strong feeling. The boy died here, in that room, along with several others in his midst, but not all at once. This made Joanna sad. He apparently escaped from somewhere, without his mom who he was waiting for, then died before they could be reunited.

Joanna would probably never know the full story, but what she knew so far made her sad. What a brave thing for a mother to do. She risked never seeing her son again just so he could be safe.

Joanna changed her focus, trying to see if she could bring the mother out. She could identify who she was, but she was still murky, in the distance somehow. Joanna listened closely and got the name, 'Jane.' There was the 'J' she was looking for.

"Jane it is," she said to herself, grabbing her notebook again and writing it down.

"Are you okay in there?" Anne said from the door.

"I'm fine," Joanna said, getting up and lifting her blanket off the floor. "I'm just talking to myself in here."

"Well, I'm surprised you haven't done that before with all that's going on here!" Anne said, following Joanna as she left the room. "Are you done in there? Can Sal close up the room?"

"I'm done," Joanna said. "Thank you, Sal," she said as he did his thing with the tapestry and the door. She looked at her watch. "Whoa! I was in there for an hour and a half? Why didn't you tell me?"

"It's no problem," Celine said. "I want to give you as much time as you need. I'm only sorry we have to do this at night at the end of all of our workdays."

"It's no problem for me," Joanna said, and Anne nodded her agreement.

"I don't care when we do this," Sal said, finishing his replacement of the tapestry, then standing back to make sure it looked okay to anyone who came near it. "I think it's interesting."

"Me, too," Anne said. "Have you been filling Sal in on all the details?"

"I sure have," Joanna said. "Me and the guys have a coffee break while I fill them all in."

"We're into it," Sal said. "My guys are getting good at keeping their mouths shut, or at least I hope they are. That's what they tell me anyway."

"We're not getting any inquiries," Celine said. "They must be."

"Good," Sal said. "The threats are working."

They all laughed.

"So are you done for tonight?" Celine asked Joanna.

"Yes, thank you, Celine," Joanna said, leading the group out to the front of the library while Celine turned off lights and shut the door to the Reference Room.

"No, thank you!" she said. "I thought I was losing my mind with all of the noises I was hearing. You've answered many questions for me and made me a firm believer in your gifts in the process. I was getting there with the Sophia case, but now I'm firmly there!"

"Any time, Celine," Joanna replied, walking out to the sidewalk with the rest of the group. Celine locked the door behind her. "Let me know when you want to come back. Goodnight all!" she said and left with a wave.

As they all got into their cars to leave, they had no idea there was someone in a car across the street watching them. Mr. Adamson, the investigation critic, had tried to get in the front door to see exactly what the group was doing, but decided to sit in his car and wait for them to come out when he pulled on the door handle and discovered the door was locked.

Unfortunately, he still didn't know exactly how they were investigating the closet or room they found, but the day before, he had quietly looked behind the new tapestry he noticed at the back of the room. He was always in the Reference Room reading newspapers or looking up random facts. He loved paper and shunned the technology of today unless he desperately needed to use it. He noticed there was a part of the wall that was cut out, carefully, but it was apparent it had been tampered with. He heard someone coming, so he laid the tapestry back where he had found it making sure it was not swinging or moving in any way. The person who entered the room was Celine, the Reference Librarian. She looked startled when she saw him in the part of the library. He had already had a book in his hand as a cover for his actions, so when she spotted him, he nodded in greeting and then returned the book to its place on the shelf.

"Hello," Ron Adamson said to her as he walked toward the door.

"Did you find what you were looking for?" Celine said.

"Oh, I most certainly did," he said and walked out the Reference Room door.

Celine had watched him go, then went over to where he had shelved the book, or rather 'mis-shelved' it. It was a high school yearbook he probably didn't even open. She knew he was the person who was against their investigation. Maybe he was looking for the door? It would be easy to find especially if you were aware that the tapestry was new. Should she let Joanna know?

She decided to leave it alone unless it seemed obvious to tell them. For now, she would worry alone.

CHAPTER 12

Thursday morning while working, Joanna's phone rang. It was Anne.

"Hey, Anne," she said when she picked up. "What's up?"

"I'm not sure you want to know," Anne began. "There's an editorial in the Voice this week."

The Voice was the City's hyper-local newspaper filled with news and information about everyone in town. It was always a place where the kids' teams were mentioned, announcements about parades and Grand Marshalls, and the odd ad for a handyman or a room for rent. It came out on Thursdays.

"OK," Joanna said, reaching for her coffee and sitting back in her chair. "What's it about?"

"You, more or less," Anne said. "Well, not by name, but it's obvious who they are talking about."

"What's it about?" she repeated.

"It talks about the library investigation and how it is a detriment to the city as well as the historic building," Anne said.

"Who wrote it?"

"That's the fun part," Anne responded. "It was written anonymously, but I can think of two people, one of which probably wouldn't bother."

"That's a loser's move," Joanna said. "If you can't say it with confidence, that means the writer has something to hide or is covering his butt. What else does it say?"

"It says we are ruining an historic building by knocking down a wall…"

"No, we're not! That's a lie!" Joanna exclaimed.

"I'm only reading what it says here," Anne said.

"What else does it say?"

"Well, this is the part you're not going to want to hear," Anne said.

"Go on," Joanna said, waiting with the phone clenched in her hand.

"It says there is an investigation run by a woman with delusions of being a psychic," Anne said.

It was quiet on the other end of the phone.

"Are you there?" Anne asked.

"I'm here," Joanna responded. "And this is exactly why I didn't want to do this. I don't want my reputation sullied, personally or professionally."

"I know, but I don't think anyone is going to listen to an editorial that isn't attributable to anyone, do you?"

"I certainly do, plus anyone around here who reads that is going to know it has to do with me after that Sophia thing," Joanna said, referring to her first case during which she reluctantly investigated and actually got an innocent man freed and the murderer arrested.

Ghostly Passage

"Think about it, Joanna," Anne reasoned. "Do you really care what the naysayers will say? Their opinion never meant much to you before."

"You're right, I hear you, but I don't like anyone talking about me like that, especially when the information is wrong," Joanna huffed. "No one is knocking down any walls. We had Sal carefully cut out that one piece with Buddy's permission."

"I know this," Anne pacified Joanna. "It has to be Mr. Adamson. That's who I think the 'anonymous' writer is.

"I agree. It has his mark all over it. Carol wouldn't have the guts to write something like that. She wouldn't want her reputation sullied like mine is being sullied now!" Joanna fumed.

"Just let it drop for now. That's my suggestion. I'm sure your agent would tell you the same."

"She would," Joanna sighed. "All right, I'll ignore it for now. Let's hope he doesn't write anything else about me."

"Let's hope," Anne agreed. "I'll drop a copy off in your mailbox when I get a moment. "Right now, I have to move on with my day."

"Thanks for letting me know about this," Joanna said.

"No problem, but really," Anne emphasized. "Don't worry about it. It's an anonymous editorial in a small town newspaper, okay?"

"Okay," Joanna responded. "I'll talk to you soon."

Joanna hung up and shook her head. After digging up the article online and reading through it, she wondered if she should approach Mr. Adamson about the editorial and what he is saying about her, but she was not certain the writer was him. She had a pretty good idea it was, though. She tried to focus on the content she was writing for a new online bakery that hired her. They specialized in pet treats such as cat cupcakes made out of ground dry cat food and dog ice cream treats. It was all truly disgusting for Joanna to envision, but that was her job sometimes. To make desirable the most undesirable product she had ever encountered. As soon as she was finished with this copy, she planned on getting back to working on her latest novel. She had most of it outlined, but she still had to tweak a few issues with the plot.

Luckily, she had just revised and submitted the copy for the pet website when the phone rang. She would not get to the book at all that day.

"Hello?"

"Ms. Davis," the male voice on the end of the line said. "This is Ron Adamson."

She sat up straight in her chair, struggling with what to say to this man who was slamming her in the press.

"Are you there?" he asked after a prolonged wait.

"I am, but I'm not sure you really want to talk to me right now," she said.

"And why would that be?"

"Because I just read that editorial you wrote about me," she replied.

"Why would you think I wrote it? And if I remember correctly, the author did not mention any names other than mentioning citizens who were defacing the library," he threw back at her.

"It would be easy for me to find out who wrote the article, so let's cut to the chase, Mr. Adamson," she said. "What is your problem with us looking into this library matter? Really, because it cannot be about defacing the library since you know no one is doing that here."

"You most certainly are and I am going to continue in my efforts to shout down your so-called investigation." He continued. "I understand you are now saying the library was an underground railroad depot which it most certainly was not."

"That's how misinformed you are, Mr. Adamson. The house that was on that site may have been, but I don't see why you take issue with all of this."

"Again, I don't want you to deface the library building," he said. "Nor do I want you bringing in looky-loos who want to hear about ghosts or souls or whatever you call them."

"No one knows about what we are doing aside from a small group of people," she assured him. "We are keeping it very close to the vest for that reason."

"Nevertheless, we are shutting it down," he said. Joanna could hear the grin on his face from the other end of the phone. "We have a City Council meeting coming up during which we will be discussing the matter."

"Wouldn't that bring attention to the investigation; attention you said you do not want?" Joanna asked. "That seems counterproductive to me."

"Hardly anyone attends the meetings aside from a few hearty souls, so I'm not worried."

"You're overconfident in your opinion," she said. "You never know who might be interested and I would rather not be known as a psychic or whatever people may call those of us who are sensitive to the other side."

"That, as you say, is your opinion, so don't show up," he said. "It's your prerogative." He paused during which Joanna had to retort. "Well, then, I'm going to hang up now. You have a lovely day." And he was gone.

Joanna had a mix of emotions going through her mind as a result of that call. Now that she wanted to know more about that little boy's situation, she did not want to stop the investigation, nor would Celine. After all, her reason for beginning at all was to find out what the noises were. How would they do that if they closed it all up? At the very least, the noises would continue and drive Celine nuts.

Joanna called Anne and filled her in. After looking up the date of the meeting on the city's website, they both decided they would be there, not as participants, hopefully, but as spectators. She was reluctant, but if she had to speak in favor of the investigation, she would do her best to portray someone who was a supporter of the library who did not see any defacement taking place.

"You're kidding me!" Julia was incensed when she heard about the meeting. "Don't these people have anything else to worry about?"

"Yeah, that was my reaction, too."

"Why would they care at all, especially if you already reassured them that you're not destroying the building and you got permission from one of the board members," Julia complained. "That should be enough."

"You're preaching to the choir, Lady," Joanna said, flipping to the following Wednesday on her Google Calendar™ and noting the meeting time.

"Are you worried about your reputation?" Julia asked. "I don't think you should."

"No, I'm over worrying about the gossips," Joanna answered, swiping a piece of lint from her desk. "I have enough of a career at this point that I don't need to worry about what small-minded folks think."

"Well, you know best," Julia said. "I would have a hard time staying away from it all, too, especially if there was a child involved like you said."

"That's what's really motivating me, even though he has already passed," she added. "I need to find out what happened."

"I know," Julia said. "Do you want me to go with you?"

"No, it's not a big deal," Joanna said. "Adamson doesn't think it will be a well-attended meeting. Besides, I'll only draw attention to myself if you go with me."

"Okay, but let me know if you change your mind," Julia replied.

"I will, don't worry," Joanna said.

"Okay, Mom. I have to go," Julia said.

"Me, too," Joanna said, turning back to her desk. "I am hardly getting any work done today other than one assignment I luckily finished before all of this drama started."

"Hang in there!" Julia said. "I'll talk to you later."

"Okay, Sweetie," Joanna replied. " 'Bye."

When Joanna hung up, it was already 4:00 and she heard the guys going past her office door. She went out to greet them and ran into Sal at the end of the line.

"Oh, good," Joanna said. "I heard they are stopping the library investigation until a City Council meeting happens next week."

"You're still getting pushback, huh?" Sal said standing at the bottom of the stairs. "We're not hurting the building."

"I'm sure there's something else going on, but I can't figure out what it is."

"There has to be," Sal agreed. "Well, just let me know when you need me and I'll be there."

"Thank you, Sal," Joanna said. "I really appreciate it. Your involvement is the reason I can confidently say we are not damaging the building. You know what you're doing."

"Thank you," he said. "I appreciate your appreciation!" He smiled and headed out to the kitchen and left by the back door as usual.

By Sunday night, the City Council meeting that had been worrying Joanna was pushed to the back of her thoughts. Margie and Jim welcomed a beautiful baby girl into the world at 3:17 in the afternoon after a long night of labor and several hours of pushing.

"She really made you work for it, huh?" Joanna said, cradling the tiny bundle in the hospital room while Margie ate dinner. She had been dying for a cheeseburger and rather than get one from the hospital cafeteria, Jim had gone to a local fast-food place that specialized in burgers.

Ghostly Passage

"It's the least I can do after all the work you did!" Jim said, eating his dinner with Margie. "Are you sure you don't want some of my fries Mom? I feel bad I didn't get you something."

"I didn't want anything," she said. "I just want to stand here and hold my new granddaughter." Joanna could not help it. She thought little Iris was beautiful, but then again, didn't all grandmothers think their grandchildren were beautiful?

"How did you come up with the name?" Joanna asked. "It's not something you hear these days."

"That's one of the reasons," Margie said. "It was also one of my great aunts' names."

"It's pretty and I like that it's different," Joanna said.

"There is also less of a chance that someone will come up with a nickname for her," Jim said, wiping ketchup from his mouth.

"Good idea," Joanna said. The baby's eyes fluttered and she opened them just as a nurse came into the room. "Hello, sweetheart," Joanna cooed. "I'm your nana."

"Oh, that's a nice name to call your grandmother," the nurse said. "I had a nana."

"So did I," Joanna said. "She's gone now, so I'm happy to take over the title."

"That's sweet," the nurse smiled, then turned to Margie. "Now did you nurse yet? Oh, I should ask first. Are you planning to nurse?"

"Yes and yes," Margie said, popping the last French fry into her mouth. "She took to it like a natural."

"That's good, because it will be less uncomfortable for you in the long run," she said. "And it gives the baby some antibodies to start off life even if you don't continue."

"I figured I would start breastfeeding and move to a bottle if she or I didn't do well with it," Margie said. "So far, so good, but I'm not making any promises."

"You do what's best for you," the nurse said. "Okay, I'm just going off shift, but Nurse Amelia will be here to take over. If you need anything at all, just push the button in that controller by the side of the bed."

"I'm good," Margie said. "Thank you for all of your help!"

"Yes, thanks," Jim said, standing to reach out his hand and shake hers.

"No problem," she said. "It's my job and I love doing it. Have a peaceful night!" she said and was gone.

"Was she the one who helped you deliver?" Joanna asked.

"Yes," Margie said, handing Jim the bag with all the trash. "She was like a drill sergeant, but in the best possible way."

Jim nodded. "I still can't believe what I saw."

"Don't hold it against me, okay?" Margie laughed.

"Yes, the mystery is completely gone, isn't it, Jim?" Joanna laughed.

"Yes, but it was amazing. What a miracle," Jim said, his eyes misting.

Margie reached for his hand and held it, then looked over at Joanna cuddling Iris. Joanna noticed.

"Oh, I'm sorry," she said. "Am I hogging the baby? Do you want her?"

"I do, but I'll have her all night," Margie said. "You hold her for a while longer."

"Just a few more minutes and then I'll let you rest," Joanna said, staring into her new granddaughter's eyes. When she did finally leave the hospital, it was with a big smile on her face. Joanna was grateful everything went okay with the birth. She had to admit she was worried after Margie's short visit to the hospital a few weeks back. Joanna encouraged Margie to take advantage of the possibility of sleep while she was still in the hospital. It would only be two days, the extra due to a slight back problem when pushing Iris out, but it was nothing serious.

Joanna got home at around 10:00. She popped her bag in her office and then headed to bed earlier than usual with the latest book she was reading. The arrival of a new baby made the world's troubles go away. Joanna wasn't going to worry about the City Council meeting now. She would just revel in the feeling of being a new grandmother. The grumps of the world could wait until tomorrow for her attention.

CHAPTER 13

Wednesday evening arrived all too soon. The meeting was scheduled for 6:00 at City Hall and Joanna arrived at 5:45 expecting to be one of only a few interested spectators. She had misjudged. When she and Anne pulled into the parking lot, they had a difficult time finding a parking space for Joanna's car. They parked way in the back corner of the lot, considering themselves lucky to get a space in the lot at all.

"There must be something else going on," Anne said, getting out of the car and meeting Joanna in roadway that led up to the side door of City Hall. "Maybe the Green has a band on tonight?"

"I don't think it's the Green," Joanna replied. "I think they hold the open-air band concerts on Fridays most of the time."

They got closer to the entrance and both women's eyes went wide. There was a line that extended just inside the double set of doors. Joanna walked up to the woman at the back of the line and asked what it was for.

"The City Council meeting," she said, still looking at her phone and never making eye contact with Joanna, which was not a bad thing. Joanna didn't want the celebrity. She and Anne stood there for another five minutes before almost everyone in line got a notification that the meeting was being moved a few blocks away to Bailey

Middle School's auditorium. Anne and Joanna shuffled back to Joanna's car with everyone else and drove to the school a few blocks away.

All of the transplanted participants made it into the auditorium and into their seats by 6:30. The Council Members took their seats onstage where a few long tables and chairs were set up, and the sound system was turned on. It was rudimentary due to the short notice, but a handheld microphone the members would pass around and another microphone on a stand for those in the audience who wished to speak would do that job.

The meeting was called to order by the Chairwoman which, Joanna noticed, was not Carol who had been nervous about the library investigation for some reason, but she was there on the stage. Joanna did not know who the woman was. She didn't recognize her and the placard she had placed in front of her was too far away.

"Do you think she'll out you for your involvement?" Anne whispered to Joanna.

"I don't know, but maybe she won't if I don't speak at all," Joanna said. "That will be difficult if things get stupid or the facts are deliberately twisted."

And after the Council went through their agenda and announced the next order of business was the library investigation, the facts were indeed twisted. Joanna watched as Mr. Adamson presented his case to the public saying the investigation was unnecessary because the group was defacing the library. He also said there was no possibility of the space being an Underground Railroad depot. During the public portion of the meeting, the crowd began to take their turn in supporting him. She knew they had read the other article about the investigation, written by interviewing Adamson, and fell for it hook, line and sinker. One after the other they spoke out against the investigation, each person less informed that the last.

Joanna could not take it anymore. She put her purse on the seat and stood at the back of the line waiting her turn to speak. She knew it was not in her best interest, but she fully believed it was the best interest for the city, the library and the little boy who speaking to her, though she kept that last fact to herself.

Before she knew it, it was Joanna's turn at the microphone. She took a breath and began.

"Good evening. My name is Joanna Davis and my address is 54 Marshall Street, West Haven."

Joanna hated giving out her address, but it was the rule of the meetings to do so for their record. She continued.

"I was asked by the library to investigate unexplained noises in the Reference Room which, as you may know, was the original library building. The library has since been built up from that original building. As you may also know, I helped with an investigation for the West Haven Police Department last year that resulted in an innocent man being freed from jail and a man who committed a murder to be prosecuted."

There was mumbling in the audience, but Joanna felt more confident as she moved forward. She knew Detective Sosa was somewhere in the audience urging her forward and she figured Sal was there, too, but she had not seen him yet. She knew these folks knew what her gifts were and it gave her confidence to continue.

"The library asked me to investigate noises at the back of the Reference Room that could not be explained. They had called an exterminator to check if squirrels or other rodents were in the wall. They had a building inspector check the safety of the structure. The noises could not be explained. I was then called to take a look at the site to give my opinion on some sort of paranormal activity."

The crowd, which had been quietly listening, began to mumble loudly. Some even called out rude comments to Joanna such as, "Sit down!" and "Freak!" Joanna kept going.

"Whether or not one believes in the paranormal or the gifts that I have, there is no need to stop the investigation. No one is defacing the library as Mr. Adamson said. We all love the building and its contents, which is the reason we bring a contractor with us each and every time. We got permission from the Library Board to carefully cut into the wall and found a door. The reason it has been such a secret undertaking was because we did not want the public to poke around and disturb the area. I would say that alone shows respect of the site. In fact, Mr. Adamson's bringing it to light in a City Council meeting is more destructive than our quiet little investigation. I hope the public respects the building as much as our small group and does not make it into a tourist destination. After all, there are still people who use the library as their quiet place to work or read. We don't want that disturbed."

Joanna paused and took a breath as she looked around the auditorium. She hoped to beseech the people there to respect the library and, in turn, their quiet investigation.

"Wouldn't you want to know what is going on? If not, why not? It doesn't hurt anyone here to have a tiny group looking into noises in the Reference Room. If we find something interesting or different, it can only benefit our city due to its historical significance. Therefore, I ask the City Council to allow us to continue our investigation." Joanna paused. "I am also happy to answer any questions you may have, but I would rather set a meeting time to do so. I fear this public forum is not the place to discuss the details."

This was followed by more mumbling as well as a few rude cat calls, but Joanna ignored them. She was focused on the Council members on the stage who were quietly discussing it amongst themselves. The crowd's reaction was the perfect illustration of her request for privacy.

"Ms. Davis," began the Chairwoman. "The Council will contact you to set up a date and time for a meeting that is mutually agreeable to us all. Please leave your contact information with me before we leave for the night. This matter is closed to public comment tonight. We reserve the privilege of reexamining the matter at a later date when we have more information at hand."

"Thank you," Joanna said and made her way back to her seat. She got a number of dirty looks and was perplexed as she made her way back to her seat in the back. Why would they be that nasty to her or about this investigation, she wondered? She guaranteed hardly any of these folks had stepped into that library in years since their last research paper in high school. If they did, it was for their children's sake and many of them would not frequent the Reference Room to research anything with Professor Google available on their phones.

Anne nodded at her as she sat down.

"Good job," she said, patting Joanna's hand.

"Let's see what happens," Joanna said, writing down her name, email address and cell phone number on a piece of paper she pulled out of a small notebook she carried in her purse.

At the end of the meeting, she walked up the side aisle to the stage and handed her information to someone that seemed to be assisting the members of the Council. He thanked Joanna and walked to the Chairwoman to give her the piece of paper. The Councilwoman looked around the man, smiled and nodded at Joanna before putting it on top of her pile of files and walking off the stage carrying everything like a student carrying her schoolbooks, her large tote balanced on her forearm.

"That was fun," Joanna smirked.

"I'm surprised you got up to speak," Anne said. "I completely understand, though. Adamson was lying through his teeth."

"He definitely was, even after I explained to him what we were doing, how we were doing it and why we were doing it."

"There may be something else going on there, don't you think?" Anne asked.

"Maybe," Joanna said, nodding to a few people who smiled at her as Anne and she walked to the car. "I'll have to do more research on the guy."

"I will, too," Anne said. "We can also ask the group to look into him."

But they did not have to ask. By the time Anne and Joanna got to Saturday's paranormal group meeting, they discovered the group was already looking into Ron Adamson.

"What made you do that?" Joanna asked, taking a seat and dropping her bag. She already had her notebook out and ready to take notes.

"We were all at the meeting Wednesday," Laura said.

"You were?" Anne exclaimed. "We didn't see any of you."

"We blend in well," Nick said. "Besides, we were scattered throughout the audience."

"We didn't want anyone to know about our group here," Sylvia said. "I also didn't think you would speak."

"We understand why you did, but I for one appreciate your not mentioning this group," Maria said to which the rest of the room nodded their agreement.

"I wouldn't do that," Joanna said. "I mean I'm not embarrassed by being here, but I don't want the naysayers to have any more ammunition with which to go at me. I also don't want to bring all of you into this, whatever it is."

"We appreciate that," Nick said. "If it gets out, it gets out, but let's try to keep it under wraps as long as possible."

"I'm doing my best," Joanna replied. "I have a meeting with the Council members this Monday afternoon."

"What are you going to tell them?" Laura asked.

"They want to know why I've been there in the first place, what we've done to the building and where this investigation is going," Joanna replied. "Celine already gave me her permission to tell them about her concerns, you know, the noises and stuff, so I'll just be as honest as possible when I answer their questions."

"Without telling them about this group?" Maria asked.

"Yes," Joanna replied. "They have no need to know about our meetings, especially if they aren't looking hard enough to find us. I mean we are on the library's schedule of room reservations, aren't we Anne?"

"Yes, but just as a social meeting," she said. "I don't give them any more information than that because they don't request it."

"That's smart," Joanna said. "So, do you all want to help me figure out why this guy has such a problem with this investigation?"

"We've already done some research on him," Nick said.

"The only thing we could find so far was that his family has been in town for a few generations," Sylvia said. "Maybe we can find something in that fact."

"Yes, I found that," Joanna said. "They owned a tobacco farm in the state but have lived in West Haven as far back as 1833. Mr. Adamson's great-great-grandfather was born here, but I couldn't find anything else before that."

"We'll help you with that," Laura said. They all caught up with their notes for a moment before Anne spoke next.

"So, now, tell everyone your good news!" Anne said.

"I'm a Nana!" Joanna said to the delight of the group which then spent the rest of the meeting talking about the pros and cons of an old-fashioned name, if the baby was keeping her parents up at night, and all manner of baby-related topics until it was time to end the meeting.

The next day, Joanna told Margie and Jim how excited her group was in hearing Iris was born.

"Oh, that's sweet of them," Margie said. She had just finished nursing and was burping Iris over her shoulder. "Do they all have kids?"

"A couple do, but I don't think anyone has a baby right now," Joanna said, taking a piece of the zucchini bread she had brought over.

"What's going on with the investigation?" Jim sat down after grabbing another cup of coffee for himself and his mother. Margie was still breastfeeding, so she didn't have any.

"I have a meeting tomorrow with the City Council members," Joanna answered.

"What do you think they are going to ask you?" Margie asked, still tapping the baby's back.

"I think they want to confirm what we are doing and if it will really hurt the library building," Joanna said.

"From what I heard, Adamson made almost everything he said up on the spot," Jim said.

"Yes, he said what he told me which was he didn't want the library defaced and there couldn't have been an Underground Railroad depot in the building," Joanna said.

"Which shows how much he doesn't know about your investigation," Jim said. "The building happens to be sitting on the house that was potentially a depot, right?"

"Exactly," Joanna said. "I've tried to reason with him, but he won't listen. The paranormal group thinks he has some other reason for stopping us."

"Maybe there's a deep dark secret in his family," Margie said. "Who owned the house that was there before the library?"

"Actually, his family did," Jim said. "I was researching it when I discovered the library was built in 1906 after slavery ended."

"I found that information and have been wondering the same thing. Did his family do something that would prevent his wanting an investigation? What could that be about?" Joanna said.

A loud belch sounded from over Margie's shoulder and they all grinned.

"That's my girl," Margie said. She wiped Iris' mouth and handed her into Joanna's outstretched arms.

"She really is beautiful," Joanna said, all the while wondering what Adamson had to hide.

"I'm not going to worry about any of that right now," Joanna smiled at her granddaughter. "I'm just going to enjoy this beautiful little lady for today." She would find out what the Council wanted the next day. She hoped they would allow her investigation to continue.

CHAPTER 14

Joanna walked into the old City Hall to the elevator, past the photographs and portraits of past mayors. This area was renovated and Joanna thought it looked very nice. From what she read, they had finally moved the Board of Education's office from an old building across town to City Hall and it was working out well.

The elevator arrived and Joanna took it up to the third floor where the Council Chambers and their offices were located. She found the office and walked in. There was no receptionist, so she called out.

"Hello?" she said and received an answer immediately. Her acquaintance, Carol, came out of one of the offices to the right.

"Hi, Joanna!" she said. "Come right into my office." Joanna followed her into a small office with two chairs placed in front of the desk. "Have a seat, would you?"

"Am I only meeting with you?" Joanna said, taking a seat and trying to be polite. "I thought the entire Council had some questions for me."

"Yes, they are making their way in from their jobs and such," she responded. "We'll be meeting in the Council Chamber because it will easily hold all of us rather than someone's cramped office."

"Okay, well, I can go in there and wait if you would like," Joanna said, about to rise and leave the office.

"No, wait," Carol said. "I wanted a quick chat with you first."

"About...?" Joanna was suspicious. Carol was vehemently opposed to the investigation right from the start. Joanna didn't like the sound of this.

"I just want to make sure you're sure you want to continue with all of this," Carol said. "You know the building was built in the early 1900's. That was after the Emancipation Proclamation, so there wouldn't have been slaves in the library at all."

Joanna took a breath. The nerve of this woman telling her the history of the building when that small piece of information was probably the only bit she knew.

Joanna remained calm.

"Do you think I don't know the history of the building, the site and the players involved in this entire situation?" Joanna asked. "As a writer for many years, I know how to research thoroughly. I also need to have my facts straight when I begin to write a word so I don't get sued. Did you know that or do you think I sit around playing all day?"

"I didn't mean..." Carol began. Joanna interrupted.

"I'm sure you didn't, but your bias is showing," Joanna said as she got up from her seat. "I'm just going to wait in the Chambers if that's okay. It's this way, right?" she said, pointing to the main door at the back of the entry room and began walking without waiting for Carol's answer.

"Yes, just through that door," Carol pointed. Joanna thought she seemed taken aback, but so was Joanna. What was her problem, and Adamson's for that matter, with checking out a room in a building for goodness sakes! It was a room that had only one door and Joanna got vibes from it, for want of a better word. She was even more invested in this investigation now that Carol had shown her colors. Perhaps it was pure stubbornness on Joanna's part, but even though he was on 'the other side,' Joanna felt a duty to this little boy. If he wanted to come out and tell her something, Joanna was going to listen.

Which is basically what she told all thirteen City Council members, all of whom showed up for a 4:00pm meeting. This surprised Joanna. Maybe they worked nearby, owned their own businesses or didn't work outside the home like Carol. She didn't know, but she did know it took a lot of convincing for the non-believers in the room. They asked why she was investigating, she told them her reasons complete with the information about the souls who have passed, and most of them turned out to be believers in the afterlife and her gifts to some degree.

"I understand you were the lady who helped the police with that cold case murder a while ago," said Jason Berg, the Council Chairperson. "Didn't you get your information from a ghost?"

"Yes, I did," Joanna replied, grimacing internally about how that sounded out loud. She continued anyway. "She appeared to me and told me the wrong man had been convicted for her murder. It turned out to be true."

"That took some guts to approach the police, I must say," Berg said, looking around at the other Council members.

"Is something similar happening in this case?" Wendy Dylan asked. "I know you said you suspect ghosts, but is that the only compelling reason to investigate this site?"

Joanna paused for a moment, thinking of the best words to use to answer without losing her audience.

"There is a little boy who continues to come forward whenever I am in the space," Joanna replied. "The information I am receiving from him is that he's looking for his mother but cannot find her."

"So these notes are true?" asked Steve Morin, another Councilperson. "There are ghosts in that room?"

"Yes, there are, and I believe many more than this little boy."

"What does that mean?" Carol asked with a smirk. "We have a haunted library?"

"Technically, yes," Joanna answered. "They were probably making noises so that someone would listen to what they needed to say."

"How would they make noises if they are, well, air?" Carol asked, looking at the other members of the Council for validation. They did not return her look. All eyes were on Joanna, waiting for her answer.

"I have no idea," Joanna said. "Someone called me because they heard noises in that area of the library and neither an electrician nor a plumber could figure out where the noises were coming from. Apparently they happened when she was alone in the Reference Room before it opened for the day and sometimes after the library doors were closed at night."

The members nodded, looking at one another as if communicating in silence. Carol looked perturbed. She realized she had lost the battle of wills. When the Council granted Joanna and her group permission to continue the investigation, Joanna sighed with relief.

"Thank you, everyone," she said. Joanna still had no clue why Carol had such a problem with the investigation. "May I ask you a question?"

"Sure," answer the Chairperson. "It seems only fair to me." The other nodded their assent.

"I am curious as to why this investigation is such a problem for Mrs. Clark," Joanna asked. There. She said it, then waited through the uncomfortable silence for her answer.

"As I said before, I am concerned about the investigation hurting the structure of the property," she said, looking a bit flustered.

"I think they have been explicit in that they are not defacing the property in any way, is that correct Ms. Davis?" Berg asked.

"Yes, it is. We have a qualified contractor with us each time we go in," Joanna explained. "We got permission from one of the Board members of the library, who got permission from the rest of the Board, to cut a small hole into the wall. When we found there was a door behind it, we got further permission to cut another hole the size of the door. It was all done carefully so as not to deface the building," Joanna said, the last bit directed at Carol, albeit unobtrusively. Carol got the message.

"Well, I think if we are all in agreement," Berg said to the group at large, "We grant Ms. Davis and her group permission to continue their investigation with careful attention to making sure they do not deface the original structure in any way."

"Thank you, Mr. Berg and Council members," Joanna said. She nodded her thanks, grabbed her purse and made for the door before Carol the opportunity to stop her. She did not think she would, but

Joanna really didn't want to speak with her right now, distrusting her mood at Carol's opposition. There was just something about her motives that Joanna didn't trust. Perhaps she, like Adamson, was hiding something which had to do with the room or the investigation. Perhaps she was just petty and wanted her own way. Joanna planned to look into a possible connection.

When she got home, she opened her email program immediately intending to email Anne and her paranormal group. Instead, one of the emails jumped out at her. It was from Ron Adamson.

Ms. Davis,

I heard you were granted access again to investigate the library. I urge you to halt your investigation. The library is an historic building which you are invading. The public will surely get wind of this and unsettle the patrons who seek a quiet spot from which to read or research when they try to view your antics. I cannot implore you strongly enough to stop investigating, close up the hole in the wall and move on to other pursuits.

Sincerely,

Ron Adamson

Joanna sat back in her chair. There had to be something else going on here, with both Adamson and Carol. Were they related? Did they have money in the game that made them urge her to stop looking into these issues at the library? She quickly forwarded the email to Anne along with detailed notes about the meeting with the Council, then began researching Adamson and more of his family's history in West Haven. She had conducted a perfunctory research session once, but now really got into it. The construction crew was gone for the day, they had been since before she left the house earlier, and she had no hard deadlines to meet at the moment. This was going to be her hard deadline, one she set for herself.

She looked up the Adamson name in the West Haven area and slowly discovered his family had lived in West Haven even before there was a West Haven when the area was called 'West Farms.' His great-great-grandfather was born there somewhere in the early 1830's. Joanna could not get the exact date of his birth, but she did discover he owned a haberdashery that kept the family well fed and clothed. Some of his children went into the business while others went to college or, in the case of the three daughters, got married to men who also had money. They bought property around town; one location was across the street from the library. This was apparently their main home where he and his wife raised their family. The house was now an historic landmark called The Savin House. Joanna had been there on field trips with her kids when they were young. She remembered it as being rather homey and comfortable, but nothing much aside from the general feeling of the place. The docents would walk around and tell you about the way people lived during that time and the furniture was accurate with regard to the era, or at least as far as she could tell.

As for Carol, she could not find much of a connection in any public records she could lay her hands on, electronically anyway, other than the usual Facebook and Instagram pages. These were filled with photos of grandchildren and her gardening results. She seemed to remember her as someone who grew up in one of the nearby cities such as Milford, but she could not be certain. She never really chatted with her on those field trips because she was always so standoffish and to herself, as if the rest of the moms and kids were not worth her time.

Nothing changed, Joanna thought, continuing to scour through the research. She didn't find much else, so she decided to take a quick look at her email so as not to get bogged down. She could easily end up for 2000 emails at the end of the week if she didn't weed out the junk a few times per week.

One subject jumped out at her. It was from a Daniel Adamson. Joanna had no idea if this was Ron using a different email or something, but she was curious. She clicked on it.

Dear Ms. Davis,

I am Ron Adamson's nephew and would like to meet with you at your earliest convenience. I work in Branford but would be happy to come into West Haven if you prefer. Please let me know the day and time that works best for you and we can set it up.

Best,

Dan Adamson

Joanna was perplexed. She had no reason to know much about Ron's family, but she did know he had a brother who she thought had already passed. Things were getting interesting.

Joanna responded she worked from home, so any time or day was good for her. She received an immediate response via email.

Would tomorrow at 11:00am be a good time to meet for coffee? Anywhere in West Haven is fine. Does Elm Diner work for you? They have the best coffee. LMK.

Dan

Joanna emailed him back and put the time on her calendar for the next day. She was excited to find out what was going on, though she suspected another play to stop the investigation. She would find out tomorrow. She picked up the phone and called Anne.

"What?" she exclaimed when she heard about the new development. "You said he's his nephew?"

"That's what he said in the email," Joanna responded, scrolling over the email with her mouse. "I'm going to go. I've already emailed back to confirm."

"Are you sure? I mean Adamson seems a little mean," Anne said. "I wouldn't trust this guy. He could be setting you up."

"What is this, a spy novel?" Joanna laughed. "No, I'll be fine at Elm Diner. There are always a lot of people there."

"Okay, but please call me as soon as you finish," Anne said. "Not only do I want to make sure you're safe, but I'm dying to know what he says."

"Me, too," Joanna said. "OK, gotta go. Have a good night."

"I will," Anne said. "I'll talk to you tomorrow."

"Okay," Joanna said and hit the button to end the call.

She decided to check upstairs to see how the work on the spare bedroom was going. Felix immediately got off the couch and followed her.

"You're really a puppy, aren't you?" Joanna said, looking back at Felix as he walked behind her up the stairs. She opened the door and saw the back wall was new. The drywall looked neat and ready to paint. She looked at the other walls. They were a pale pink color, not necessarily a color Joanna wanted to repeat. This had been Julia's room when she lived home. She had been on her own for years, so maybe this was a good time to change colors. Since the bathroom was blue, she thought maybe a light green might work, like her favorite scarf. She would take a look at paint on her way to her meeting on Saturday, just so it was ready when Sal was ready.

Joanna wondered who he would hire to paint now that Squirrel was in jail. That's why she hired Sal, though. It was up to him to figure out whom to hire to paint the room. Joanna did not have to worry about it.

She left and closed the door behind her, wondering what the next day with Dan might reveal.

It turned out the next day revealed a lot of new information Joanna did not have before. When she walked into the diner, Dan was seated at a booth in the back near the pastries. Unfortunately he was facing the door, probably so he could see her coming in. This meant Joanna had to deal directly with the temptation of the yummy pastries all through her meeting.

"It's a pleasure to meet you," Dan said, standing to reach out a hand to shake.

"You as well," she said, returning the handshake. She sat down and put her purse to the side on the seat. They both gave their order to the waitress before Joanna started.

"So, to what do I owe this honor?" she asked.

"I'm sure it was quite a surprise to hear from anyone named Adamson," he said, toying with the place setting in front of him.

"It was," she said, taking in his neat button-down shirt and curly brown hair. She guessed he was about 45. "Are you here to reinforce your uncle's warnings?"

"No, no," he said quickly. "I think you should investigate the building."

The waitress brought two cups of hot coffee and then left to check on other patrons of the diner. Joanna took a sip.

"So, why am I here?" she asked, then realized how rude that sounded. "I'm sorry to sound rude. Your uncle has been bullying me to stop investigating the library, so I'm surprised you are in favor."

"I completely understand," he replied. "I was at his house the other day and he couldn't stop complaining about it. I tried to reason with him, but he is stuck on stopping you."

"He has to have something to hide, if I may say so."

"He does," Dan said. Joanna stopped her cup midway to her lips and then put it back on the saucer.

"What do you mean?" she said. Dan pulled a small book out of his backpack and slid it across to Joanna.

"What is this?" she asked, looking at it as if it were about to be detonated.

"It's a journal," he answered. "Of my family. I took it from my uncle's bookcase when I was there the other day."

"Tell me more," she commanded, reaching a tentative finger to touch the cover. It felt like old leather and was well-used.

"The family-owned tobacco farms and a store a few generations ago," he said, telling Joanna what she already knew, but did not want to admit she knew. It would make her look like a stalker. Instead, she waited for Dan to continue.

"My three-time-great grandfather was born here before it was even West Haven," he said, then noticed her expression. "But you already know the basics, don't you?"

Joanna blushed. "Yes, I have to admit I do. I had to do a little research to see who I was dealing with, didn't I?"

"Fair enough," he said, and then continued. "He doesn't know I 'borrowed' that journal, so I would appreciate your keeping that to yourself and returning it without his finding out I gave it to you."

"What am I looking for when I read it?" Joanna said, picking up the book and giving it a cursory flip-through while she waited for Dan to answer.

"The answer to some of your questions," he said. Dan took a deep breath and ploughed forward with his explanation. "It seems someone in the family had slaves ..."

"What? We're in the north the last time I checked," she said. "Did the state line change without the history books recording it?"

"No, that's one of the problems," he said.

"*One* of the problems?" she asked.

"Yes," he said, taking a sip of his coffee. "It appears the two former slaves he had working for him, without pay, threatened to tell authorities and he didn't like that."

"Well, of course, but why didn't they tell someone anyway?"

"Because slave catchers could still catch them and bring them back down south if they found them," Dan said, watching Joanna's surprised look.

"I had no idea," she said. "I thought they were free once they got here."

"No, they were not. The slave catchers were mercenaries who would hunt escaped slaves and return them to their owners for a reward."

"And so why did your ancestor have two slaves?" Joanna asked. She felt as if she was in the middle of a mystery novel. It got worse.

"He owned a tobacco farm a few miles from here and needed the help," Dan said. "He also had them work around the house a bit. Apparently they lived in the attic rooms of his house."

"Why didn't anyone else give them up? The people that worked with them on the farm?"

"I'm not sure," Dan said. "His journal there doesn't say, but I imagine they were paid a little extra to keep it quiet. Plus they needed the help. Tobacco growing is labor intensive when it is time to harvest, or that's what I've read in my own research."

"The farm must have been big?"

"Yes, quite a lot of acreage from what I gather," Dan said, taking another sip of his tepid coffee. He motioned for the waitress to warm his cup. She had been walking around with the pot, so she came right over to pour more into each of their cups.

"I sense there is more to this story," she said, taking a sip.

"There certainly is," he said and let the story unfold.

Dan's three-time-great grandfather did not like the threat from the two male slaves. He had not had any children by 1862, so it had been rather easy to keep his activities quiet.

"John Adamson was not a nice man," Dan continued. "He paid someone to murder both of them."

"But how could he have gotten away with that?" Joanna exclaimed. "And what does that mean to this investigation?"

"He also owned the house that stood on the lot where the library stands now," he said.

Joanna's eyes got big; her coffee completely forgotten at this point. "He lived there?"

"No, his parents lived in the house, but at that point they seemed to be infirm and died within close proximity to one another also in 1862."

"So…?" Joanna was getting aggravated with Dan's pace while storytelling. She wanted him to get to the point and he sensed that.

"There was a root cellar at the back of the house," Dan said. "He buried them in it."

"What? Are they there now?" she asked.

"I believe so," he said.

"But I never saw anything that looked like a root cellar in that room," she said, scouring her memory of the space in question.

"It was apparently right outside the back door," he said. "That door you found was probably the back door of the kitchen."

"Oh my goodness," Joanna said, now eager to read the journal Dan had just handed her. "But what about the little boy that keeps appearing? Did you hear about the little boy?"

"I did, but I'm not sure the two are completely connected," Dan said. "From what I've read, the housekeeper and her husband who was the gardener or landscaper or something, may have indeed run a depot for escaping slaves without my great-great whatevers knowing about it."

"Wouldn't they have known about the bodies then?" Joanna asked.

"No because John Adamson ordered the landscaper to seal the root cellar," he said. "He mentions how annoying it was that the landscaper did not simply follow his orders when he told him to do so and gave him pushback. Apparently his wife, the housekeeper, wanted him to go down and see if they left any of the food down there before they sealed the entry shut, not that she planned to use it. Earlier in the journal he wrote that the canning, potatoes and such had been relocated to another root cellar built on the side of the house, farther away from the kitchen door." Dan paused. "I couldn't figure out where exactly. Maybe you can find that."

"So the landscaper unknowingly sealed the grave of these two poor people whom your ancestor murdered?"

"Exactly," Dan said. "I'm sorry to tell you all of this, but I think my uncle knows this and doesn't want his name tarnished should you discover the details."

"He made it clear he is not a believer, so this seems like it fits, yet doesn't."

"He's probably just telling you he's not a believer and using the defacement story as a cover," Dan said. "If he stops the investigation, no one will find out about this murder way back in the 1800's."

Ghostly Passage

"I can't wait to read through this and then visit the site again with this new information," Joanna said.

"Please don't let anyone know we spoke," Dan pleaded.

"I've already told one of my group members who has been helping me, but I can swear her to secrecy," she admitted.

"Will she keep quiet?" Dan asked, his face a mask of worry.

"Definitely," Joanna asked. "Rest assured, your secret is safe with me." Joanna grabbed her purse and stuffed the notebook inside. "Thank you very much for giving this to me. I know it takes courage to go against your family if you think they are wrong."

"It does, and I may have to tell him about my involvement anyway, but I'll wait. Can you keep me updated please?" Dan asked. "You can email me when you need to. I check it several times a day."

"I certainly will," Joanna said. She stood up and put out her hand. "Thank you again for calling me," she said, shook his hand and walked out of the diner. She couldn't wait to call Anne and tell her what just happened, but first she texted Celine.

Can I get into the library tonight to investigate?

It took only a moment to get a response.

'See you at 8:15.

She set up her phone in her car and dialed Anne as she drove home, eager to read the journal once she got there.

"Are you kidding me?" Anne said, the excitement evident across the line.

"I am going back to the library tonight," Joanna said. "I need to see if I can find any evidence of that root cellar."

"Can Sal get there tonight?"

"I'm sure he can, but I'll ask him when I get home," she replied. "I'll confirm with you later this afternoon. I can't wait to curl up with this journal!"

"I don't doubt that," Anne said. "I'll talk to you later."

When Joanna arrived home, she heard the guys upstairs talking and joking with one another. She dumped her bag in her office and went up to find Sal.

"Hey," he said when he saw her through the door. "We're almost finished here. You just have to pick out the paint and I'll set up a painter to come in unless you want wallpaper again."

"No, paint is good," she responded. "I was going to choose a color over the weekend. Is that okay with you or do you want me to do it sooner?"

"No, the weekend is fine," he said. "We still have a few things to finish here."

"Can I talk to you out here for a minute?" she asked, guiding Sal down the stairs to the foyer.

"Anything wrong?" he asked.

"No, I just need you at the library tonight," she said. "Will that work for you?"

"As far as I know," he said. "I'll say yes and let you know if my wife has plans for me." He took out his phone from his back pocket and looked up his wife's number.

"I really appreciate it, Sal," she said. "I feel bad I'm always taking you away from your family."

"Don't worry about it," he replied. "Andrea doesn't mind. She thinks it's interesting."

"Well, tell her I appreciate her giving up time with you for this."

"I will," he said, then looked at his phone. "And just like I suspected, she has no problem with me being there tonight."

"Thank you," she said. "I'm getting some coffee and I won't even ask if you guys want some."

"Yep, we always bring our own," Sal said, chuckling as he went back to work and Joanna headed the other way for her coffee. When the coffeemaker burped the last of the hot liquid, she grabbed her cup and went into her office. She still couldn't believe Dan had lifted his uncle's journal and then given it to her to borrow! Was this some sort of crime she wondered? No, it was a family heirloom that Dan had the right to 'borrow.'

She began at the beginning, reading about farm transactions and the daily life of John Abramson for several pages. It was interesting to read about life in another era. Then she got to the part that confirmed what Dan had told her. Joanna was surprised his ancestor would write out that someone was murdered, but there it was. Perhaps he had not expected to die before burning the book, but he had and her it all was, laid out for everyone to see.

"How dumb," Joanna murmured to herself. It wasn't even in code! He wrote about the two slaves' threat to turn him in to the authorities and their demand for some sort of pay for their work, his refusal, and then a few days later they were gone. He did not name the person he had kill them but made an obvious reference to the $500 he paid the person who killed them and then another $200 for him and a friend who agreed to bury them both in the root cellar. 'Bury' was not the right word when they basically dumped them in there and then closed the door. While mentioning the landscaper who he ordered to seal off the door, he spoke more of his annoyance that the man was discussing it with him and not just doing as he asked, no demanded. No one else went in the root cellar-turned-tomb again after that.

The new root cellar must have been dug up when the city built the basement of the new section of the library, so that could not be confirmed. The original root cellar, however, could. Joanna was eager to get to the library that night and filled her time waiting by finishing her reading of the journal. It was fascinating.

CHAPTER 15

Joanna met Anne at the door of the library just as Celine was opening the door for them. Celine stepped back, let them in and locked it behind them.

"Mr. Lawson is here," Celine said leading them up the stairs.

"How did he even know we were coming tonight?" Anne asked.

"I think he has a sixth sense about knowing when we're going to do this," Celine replied. "He called me this afternoon to ask when we were meeting again and I told him."

"Well, that's okay," Joanna said. "He's not one of the naysayers."

"No, I think he believes in all of this," Celine said, opening the door to the Reference Room.

"Hello there!" Buddy said, standing up from his seat at one of the tables and extending his hand to first Joanna and then Anne. "I hope I'm not in the way, but I find all of this fascinating."

"I appreciate that!" Joanna said, dropping her bag on a chair.

"So, what are you going to do tonight?" Buddy asked.

"More of the same," Joanna said, stopping when they all heard a knock at the front door. Celine excused herself to see who it was and came back with Sal.

"Hi, everyone," he said. "Am I late?"

"Not at all. Right on time." Anne said. "We appreciate your being here to make sure we aren't 'defacing' the library."

Sal grinned. "Not with me on the job," he said, walking over and pulling the tapestry back and jiggling the piece of wall covering the door. "Do you want me to open the door for you?"

"Yes, please," Joanna said. As he did that, she told the others a little of what she had found. "I was given a journal from someone who shall remain nameless. It details a crime that may explain what's been going on here." Joanna held up the book she had just taken out of her purse.

"Really?" Buddy asked. "What kind of crime?"

"I would rather not say at this point," Joanna said flipping through the journal to a page she had marked earlier that day. It would give her a clue as to where to start looking. "I need to go in there again and look for a disturbance in the dirt floor."

"Wow, this *is* getting interesting," Buddy said.

"I'll say," Sal said, pulling open the door and stepping back. "Go for it. Do you need help?"

"Do you think if I tap the floor I'll find it?"

"I don't know what you're looking for, but if anything is different, you should be able to hear it," Sal responded. "Here. Take my carpenter's ruler." The yardstick folded and Sal unfolded it to its full length. "It won't bend unless you click it back into place. Just tap on the dirt and you may hear a difference."

"Thanks, Sal," Joanna said and took it from him. "I'm just going to sit there for a bit before I start tapping on the ground." Joanna left the journal on the table, got the blanket she had brought with her and went through the door, laying the blanket on the floor again a few feet from the door.

She sat down, opening her channels and trying to hear whatever the souls wanted to tell her. First the little boy came and almost stood before her. He didn't say anything or impart any information. Then the energy changed. It was not bad, just different. It was as if the boy stepped aside and another, older, soul stepped forward. The image she got was of a tall male. He didn't say anything that she could hear or feel, so she just sat there and waited. Suddenly Joanna had the feeling she should go to a certain spot and start tapping. She got up and went over to a spot about six inches from where she was seated. With the ruler, she tapped. She tapped on a spot about two feet in length along the side wall and then came back. She repeated that on an area about a foot out from the wall and followed the same path. Nothing.

While she was doing that, she could not help but feel a presence where she had been sitting. She stopped tapping, closed her eyes and tuned in. It was the boy again. She could hear the group outside the door whispering while she sat down on the blanket again but decided if the boy wanted to tell her something, she would listen.

He gave her a lot of information this time, or rather, his mother did, but from a distance through the boy. The impressions came quickly. She hoped she would remember them all.

The boy's mother could not continue the journey and passed him off to a kind woman who was traveling north with the group he was in. The mom could not continue because she was being hunted, not just because her owner suspected she was escaping, but because her husband did something to the owner or another person who was not a slave. Joanna continued to listen closely. She got an image of the mother running with the boy, holding his hand, but almost dragging him along. At one point, when she seemed to think it was safe enough, she bent down and hugged the boy. Joanna thought of the phrase, "to hug the stuffing out of someone." This is exactly the feeling or impression Joanna got. The woman didn't want to let him go but had to so he would survive.

He did not say anything, probably having been conditioned not to because of the way he lived, but Joanna had the impression the tears were rolling down his cheeks like crocodile tears. She stopped to confirm this with the boy and he confirmed her impressions.

It was almost as if Joanna was watching a movie, but it was more like impressions in her mind or strong feelings as if she was the one experiencing the feelings for herself, in her own body.

Joanna tuned back to the images unfolding. She lost the trail of the mother but got the distinct impression she never escaped. Obviously she was dead by now some one hundred plus years later, but Joanna got the feeling she lived on the same plantation or farm for the rest of her life.

As for the boy, the soul who stood before her was little. He had died young before he could move on to the next depot. She wanted to make sure, so she asked him once again.

"Yes!" he said, confirming her suspicions. Joanna listened closely and understood he passed from a high fever. He showed her being hot, then cold and shivering no matter how much clothing or cloth was piled on him. He did not tell her how long it lasted, but Joanna's impression was that he was only sick a short time before he died.

She waited to hear more. Why was he here? Where was he buried? He told her he did not know where he was buried, but this was the last place he had lived, so he just stayed after he died.

Joanna could still feel the other souls in the background but was glad she got the answers about this boy. She still would not be able to find out who he was, but she was glad she at least had a name.

Joanna shook her head. She was wiped out and the souls she was talking to seem to sense that. Maybe, she thought, her channels closed or somehow stopped working when they were overloaded. She did not know, but she did know she was finished for the evening.

"I think we need a more professional look at the floor," Joanna said coming out of the door to the group that waited.

"Can I ask what you're looking for?" Buddy asked. "It would make it easier to figure out what you need."

"I'm looking for a covered root cellar," Joanna said, then stopped when she heard Mr. Adamson's voice by the door.

"You are not digging anything up!" he said advancing on the group. "I said I do not want you defacing this library."

"Well, that's all well and good, Ron, but I've given them permission as has the City Council," Buddy said, turning to Mr. Adamson. "I can assure you, once again, that they are not defacing the library in any way. They are just looking around."

"They don't need to look around," Adamson said. "I've heard they think this was a depot on the Underground Railroad and I assure you it was not. This was my family's land before the library was built and I do not want anyone doing anything to it beside closing that door and covering it up again."

"And why would that be, Ron? What is the problem with people looking around?" Buddy paused and looked at Mr. Adamson. "What exactly are you trying to hide?"

"Nothing at all," Mr. Adamson replied, though he seemed slightly rattled. "I'm not trying to hide anything, I'm just worried about the building."

As he said this, Joanna realized he must know about the journal. She then realized it was lying on the table, but she could not get to it without drawing attention to it. She had to hope Mr. Adamson did not realized what it was while he blustered.

"I'm not sure you have a leg to stand on Ron, and I am asking you to leave," Anne said moving to the side of Buddy Lawson to block Adamson's view of the table and thus the journal. "We have permission, we have a licensed contractor approved by the Council, and we have Mr. Lawson here with us." Buddy took the opportunity of her pause to interject.

"Anything else Ron?" he said.

"You'll be hearing from me," Adamson said. He looked like he was doing a scene from a bad old movie. He then turned and stalked out of the library.

"I had better lock the door behind him," Celine said, leaving the room. "Carry on without me!" she called over her shoulder.

"So, what's next?" Buddy asked Joanna. "Do you have any ideas about how to find this hidden root cellar?"

Ghostly Passage

"I do," she said. "I've been reading up on this type of thing and it seems as if a metal detector might be the best thing to use."

"Why a metal detector?" Anne asked while Celine returned to the room.

"A metal detector will detect nails, cans or other metal object that might have been in the root cellar," she said. "You see, it would have eventually collapsed with time. Objects would have been buried by the dirt and debris when that happened."

"That makes sense. You might find lids to jars, nails, whatever," Sal said. "I may have someone who might do it for you."

"That would be perfect, Sal," Joanna said. "I'll pay them for their time."

"No, you won't," Buddy said. "The library will pay since it's technically for us that you are conducting this investigation."

"Thank you, Mr. Lawson," Celine said. "I know this has been a pain in the neck for everyone, but I really appreciate your support, and the Board's support. I tried to figure out where the noises were coming from in the usual ways, but there were no answers. This is giving us so much more information, even if some people do not believe it."

"I'm a believer, I assure you," Buddy responded. "Many of the Board members are as well."

"That's good to know," Joanna said, heading back into the empty closet to retrieve her blanket. She handed the ruler back to Sal with her thanks when she got out again. He refolded it, stuck it in his toolbox and got on with closing the door and recovering the area with the tapestry.

"So, do you know someone with a metal detector willing to go in there with Joanna?" Anne asked.

"I think so," he said. "I'll ask around quietly and get back to you guys within a day or two."

"Thanks, Sal," Buddy said, reaching out to shake his hand. "I know we all here really appreciate your help."

"I certainly do," Joanna said. "It lends credibility to our little project in that it proves we are doing our best to take care of the building and not deface it in any way."

"No problem, people," he said, picking up his tools. "And with that, I'm going home to my wife. Have a great night."

"We'll follow you so Celine doesn't have to make two trips," Anne said. She saw Joanna's startled look when she realized the journal was no longer near her purse on the table and whispered to her. "I've got it."

Joanna knew what she was talking about and let out a big breath of relief while she took the book from Anne and stowed it in her bag.

"Thank you," she whispered back as they all made their way out of the room and out of the library with Celine closing the door behind her.

"Thank you again, everyone," Celine said. "Let me know when you find that person with the metal detector and we can do this again."

"I appreciate it, Celine," Buddy said. "Thank you."

"Okay, thank you all around," Anne said, smiling, but assertive. "Let's go before people wonder what our small crowd is doing in front of the library at this hour."

Everyone agreed and went to their cars. On the drive home, Joanna couldn't help but wonder what they would find when they got digging. That was if they dug at all. They would have to wait to see what the metal detector discovered.

CHAPTER 16

"Hello cutie!" Joanna said as Margie walked in the door a couple of days later. "Why didn't you call me? I would have come to you?" she told her as she took Iris' carrier from Margie.

"I needed to get out of that house," Margie answered. "I didn't want her to go out in public yet, so I figured I would come visit you. Are you working?"

"Yes, I am, but there is always time for a break to see my little granddaughter," Joanna said, reaching into the baby carrier to unlatch Iris from the car seat that acted as a carrier as well. Iris remained asleep as Joanna cradled her and led Margie into the kitchen.

"Are you drinking coffee or are you still breastfeeding?" Joanna asked, the fact that Margie may not want caffeine suddenly dawning on her.

"No and ye, but I fed her before we got in the car and I'd kill for a little boost right now," Margie said. "I'll only drink half a cup."

"You do look tired, but it will pass," Joanna said, popping a capsule of her strongest coffee into the machine. "How is breastfeeding going, if I may pry?"

"Iris is a pro at it and I am making more than enough milk for her," Margie said.

"I assume you're taking advantage of that and pumping every now and then so you can store it?" Joanna asked.

"I certainly am," Margie said. "I think that's why it's coming in so well. When I realized there would be more than enough, I started pumping and giving Jim the middle-of-the-night feeding when he's not too tired himself."

"That's a great idea," Joanna said, placing a cold glass of water in front of Margie along with her coffee. She usually loved a cup of black coffee, but not when she was still breastfeeding. A half of a cup wouldn't hurt Iris. "I remember John rarely got up when the kids were little. I felt guilty because he had to work, so I absolutely never slept."

"Not a chance that's happening in our house," Margie said, sipping her coffee with delight. "Iris is his baby, too."

"I completely agree with you," Joanna responded.

"He hangs out with her when he comes home while I cook dinner or just so I get a break," Margie smiled. "It's so cute watching them together when he doesn't see I'm watching."

"It's special, isn't it?"

"It is," Margie said and guzzled most of her glass of water. "Mm-mm. I didn't realize how thirsty I was!"

"I think everything tastes good when you're nursing and when you're pregnant," Joanna said, sipping her coffee.

"I think so," Margie said, taking another appreciative gulp of her coffee after putting her glass of water down. "So what's going on with that investigation? I heard Adamson barged in the other night."

"Word certainly travels fast around here," Joanna mused. "What did you hear?"

"One of the moms at the pediatrician's office recognized me as your daughter-in-law and felt compelled to tell me he barged in on your investigation Tuesday night," Margie said.

"Yes, he did," Joanna said. "It was as if he was listening in to our conversation, looking for something to pounce on."

"What did he pounce on?"

"Oh, you didn't hear that too?" Joanna grinned.

"No, just that he barged in. So what happened?"

"He came in when he heard we wanted to check out the floor to see if there's a root cellar down there," Joanna said.

"What do you want to do, dig up the floor? Didn't you say it was made of dirt?" Margie asked, leaning over to wipe Iris' mouth with a burp cloth she had over her shoulder. Iris continued to snooze away.

"I was tapping it with a big ruler. Sal has to see if it was any different than the rest of the floor," Joanna replied. "Very carefully I might add."

"Did you find anything?" Margie asked, her eyes wide with curiosity.

"No, so we want to get a metal detector in there to see if we find anything," Joanna said.

"I would think you'd find metal in pipes or electrical wires or something, no?" Margie asked.

"No because there is nothing underneath this part of the building," Joanna said. "It's just dirt, but it was there when the original house was there."

"So what kind of metal are you looking for?"

"If it was the root cellar I'm looking for, it might have lids from jars or Sal thinks there may be nails and other pieces of metal."

"May I ask why you are looking for a root cellar anyway?" Margie asked.

"Well," Joanna began, and told her all about the journal, Dan and the potential murders. Margie was an eager audience enjoying a mystery of sorts while, unfortunately, Iris slept on through the entire visit, not even waking when her Nana kissed her and put her in the carrier for the ride home.

"I'm sorry she didn't wake up for you," Margie said. "Maybe I should have jiggled her foot a little so she would wake up and say hello to her grandmother."

"That's all right," Joanna said, admiring the beautiful new addition to her family. "I never like to wake a baby anyway. She would cry and that's not a good look for me, is it? I don't want her to associate me with someone who interrupts her naptime."

While Joanna was seeing Margie out, Sal appeared at the top of the stairs.

"Is that the baby?" he asked eagerly and began quickly running down the stairs. Mario and Rob right behind him when they heard the word, "baby."

Margie doubled back and took the admiration as her due while the three men cooed at and admired Iris, trying to wake her up.

"Boy, she's a sound sleeper!" Sal said. "Does she sleep through the night yet?"

"Not at all, but I don't want to wake her during the day when she's still so little," Margie said.

"You're going to have to when she's a little bigger so she gets used to sleeping through the night," Mario said.

"Yeah, that's what we did with all three of our kids," Rob said. "Otherwise, like you said, you'll never get a good night's sleep."

"Don't worry," Margie said, lifting the baby carrier. "I'm only giving it a few more weeks and then I'll limit the naps."

"Congratulations!" Sal said and the other two men seconded that.

"Thank you," Margie said. The crew went back upstairs to work as Joanna walked Margie to her car.

"Do you need anything?" Joanna asked. "Diapers? Formula or anything?"

"No, I'm good, Joanna," Margie said, stepping aside so Joanna could say goodbye to Iris after she clicked the baby carrier into the base in the car.

"I'll bring over dinner tomorrow night so you don't have to cook. How's that?" she asked, cooing at her granddaughter who was still asleep. "It will be a nice way to end the week. Maybe you'll get a good night's sleep with one less thing to do."

"Now that I would appreciate," Margie said. "They're so little, but so exhausting at the same time."

"I know it," Joanna said, reaching out to hug Margie. "I promise it will get better. When you're ready for a date with my son, call me and I'll babysit for you. Okay?"

"That's another offer I'll take you up on," she said. "Will you close the door after I start the car for me? It's too hot out today."

"Certainly," Joanna said, then did so when Margie started the car and cracked the window a good few inches. Joanna waved as Margie pulled out and then headed back to her office to work. Today was a bunch of short pieces for a catalog company with work on her next novel after that. It was sure to take her mind off the little boy and the investigation for a few hours.

That night, the little boy appeared in her dream. Joanna had always thought when you saw the eyes looking at you in a dream, it was the person who had passed paying the dreamer a visit. That is exactly what happened. Joanna looked into the eyes of a young boy, the same boy she had been investigating, before he started wandering around looking for something. All at once, he found the person he was looking for – his mother. Joanna somehow knew it was his mother instinctively as dreams tend to go. He reached out his hands to her as she reached back to him. The woman picked up the boy and cuddled him in her arms as if she never wanted to let him go.

Joanna woke up at this point in the dream and reached for the notebook she kept in her bedside table so she could write down all of her impressions. She had already gotten the feeling the boy had already found his mother on the other side. This dream just reinforced that. Maybe, she thought, that was the reason she had it. Regardless,

Joanna wrote it all down, ready for her paranormal group meeting tomorrow. When she was done, she closed the notebook, stowed the pen in the coiled spine, and turned off the light.

This dream wasn't ominous and didn't keep her up like the ghostly visits did in the past when Sophia was looking for her murderer. And she wasn't experiencing the chanting she used to experience during that time. She had eventually had a priest into her house to bless it as well as a shaman to sage it for her. One could never be too careful in her opinion. In fact, Joanna fell back asleep knowing the boy had eventually been reunited with his mother, no matter how his life ended here on earth.

It was a peaceful sleep that Joanna welcomed.

Joanna got the okay for the visit from the detectorist, which is what, she learned, the person who used the metal detector was called. Sal called right before she left for her paranormal group meeting and said Joseph, the detectorist, was available whenever she wanted to go. This was exciting news and she couldn't wait to tell the group.

"Hi, everyone!" she called out as she got to a seat, apparently the last one to arrive.

"I've filled them all in on our last visit to the site," Anne said.

"Ooh, fancy! It's 'the site' now, is it?" Joanna joked while she placed her bag beside her seat and took out her notebook.

"That sounds so cool, finding a root cellar," Laura said. "Why are you looking for it? I mean, what exactly does it say in the journal to make you want to find it?"

Joanna glanced at Anne unobtrusively, not wanting to let anyone else in on their discovery that Abramson's ancestor had committed murder and stuffed the bodies there, so she was vague in her answer.

"Oh, I just figured if the room was built over where the back door used to be, that's where we might find a root cellar," she answered.

"What's the metal detector going to look for?" Nick asked.

"I would imagine there might be lids to canning jars or nails from the building of the library or the demolition of the old house," Joanna answered. "It was the contractor's idea, but we figured it was worth a try."

"I think so," Nick said. "People use metal detectors to search around old outhouses, too. That's where people would dump their trash. When it was filled, they just covered it over and moved to another site."

"That sounds disgusting," Sylvia said. "Interesting but disgusting."

"Well, let's hope we don't find an outhouse there and it's only a root cellar," Anne added. She paused and looked around the group. "Has anyone else had anything happen in the past week?"

They all remained quiet for a time before Joanna inched up her hand.

" 'Sorry,' " she said. "Me again if no one has anything else?" she asked.

The chorus of affirmative responses spurred Joanna forward.

"I had a dream last night, and it included the boy I've been investigating and his mother," she said. Every eye was wide as they listened to the contents of her dream, how she saw his eyes, and the impression she made it home to his mother.

"So, you think if you see someone's eyes in a dream that they're directly reaching out to you?" Maria asked.

"I do," Joanna said. "I know it sounds crazy, but I've had it happen in dreams before. It feels different than a regular dream."

"I don't disagree," Maria responded. "I've had similar experiences with my dreams over the years."

"I think it's given you some closure with regard to the little boy," Anne said, smiling at Joanna.

"I also got word that we have our metal detector person," Joanna said. "Sal called me last night and told me it's all set. We can set up a meeting whenever we want."

"Oh, that's good," Anne said. "We can talk to Celine to set it up before we leave."

"I hate to ask, but do you think she'll let us come this time?" Laura asked. It seemed as if the entire group leaned forward in their seats while they waited for her answer.

"I'll see what I can do when we speak with her today," Joanna said. "I'm sure she won't mind since Mr. Lawson is on board."

"As long as you don't make it too obvious," Anne said. "You have to wait until 8:15 after the library closes for the day, you can't bunch up on the street or in the parking lot when we come out, and you need to be aware of the librarian's reluctance to make a big deal out of all of this."

"Even though it actually is a big deal?" Nick asked and the others chuckled.

"Yes," Anne said. "We're working around her schedule."

"Not a problem. I'm sure we can all behave," Laura said, directing her comment to Nick.

The others nodded and agreed to Anne's terms.

"I'll text the group and let you know when we're going in with the metal detector," Joanna said. "Does that sound good to everyone?"

Again, the group agreed and talked about Sylvia's haunted house for the rest of the meeting. After they broke for the week, Anne and Joanna went to visit Celine in the Reference Room.

"Monday night works for me," Celine said as she shelved books around the library. "As long as it's still okay with Mr. Lawson."

"Oh, it's fine," Anne said. "So we'll see you Monday night after closing as usual."

"I'll see you then!" Celine said, heading into the stacks.

"What do you think about my dream?" Joanna asked Anne as she held the door for her.

"What do you mean?"

"I mean did the boy follow me home? Should I sage the house or call another priest?" Joanna asked.

"You are too funny," Anne grinned. "Yes, he probably actually came to you in a dream, but he's not a bad entity, is he?"

"No, but..." Joanna began.

"Then I wouldn't worry about it," Anne said. "Just be happy he came to you to tell you he was all right."

"Okay," Joanna said getting into her car. "I'll see you Monday."

" 'See ya!" Anne said before backing out of her spot and leaving the library parking lot.

Joanna left and went home to sage her house anyway. After what happened with the other ghost in her house, she wasn't taking any chances.

"Are you going to tell Abramson what you know?" Julia asked when she called Joanna later in the day.

"Not yet," Joanna replied. "I'm going to wait until we actually have something, after the detectorist gets in there."

"That's still such a funny word," Julia said. "It says it like it is, but it's just weird."

"A little bit," Joanna said and coughed for the fifth time since she picked up the phone.

"Why are you coughing?" Julia asked. "Are you getting sick?"

"No, I'm smudging the house with sage," she responded, and then filled Julia in on the dream, the ghost and her fears while she continued with her task.

"I think Anne is right," Julia said. "I don't think a dream means he followed you home. He was probably just letting you know he was okay like Anne said."

"Yeah, but after all of the chanting last time, I am not taking any chances," Joanna said, running the sage stick around the front door and closing it before putting out the stick in a small shell filled with sand from the beach.

"Your house must smell like weed after that!" Julia chided.

"It sure does," Joanna said, placing the shell and its contents on a shelf on one of her bookcases and plopping down on the couch. She pet Felix while she chatted. "I wonder what Sal and the guys think when they come in here after one of my little impromptu smudge sessions."

"They probably think you smoke weed!" Julia laughed.

"Probably!" Joanna said.

"Are you doing anything tonight?" Julia asked.

"I plan to change into my pj's and get comfy with a book," Joanna responded. "You?"

"Nothing at all, which is what I wanted this week," Julia said. "It's been a killer with openings in ten different cities." Julia's company had cosmetic counters at malls around the world, but the company was just trying out a standalone presence in various big cities in the United States. As such, Julia's work was more taxing than if they were opening a regular counter in a regular department store like they had done for many years. They'd had to change strategies since the malls were closing or had already closed.

"I get it," Joanna said. "You have a wonderful, quiet evening and I will do the same."

"I promise you I will," Julia replied. "I love you, Mom!"

"I love you back!" Joanna said and disconnected the call. She went in search of her book, some dinner for one and a quiet Saturday night.

CHAPTER 17

Monday morning dawned bright and sunny, the cicadas informing the world it was late August in Connecticut. Joanna was sitting on the front porch drinking her first cup of coffee of the day when a car drove up and parked in front of her house. An older woman with gray hair and a flowered skirt and blouse got out and approached Joanna.

"Are you Joanna Davis by any chance?" she asked.

"Yes, I am," she said, standing up and putting her coffee down. "May I help you with anything?"

"Actually, I may be able to help you," she said. She reached out her hand to shake. "I'm Gert Brewer from the Savin House."

"It's nice to meet you," Joanna said taking her hand. "I have to admit I haven't been to see it yet since it was renovated. My kids went there several times for school field trips and I chaperoned. It's been that long. My kids are grown up now.."

"That's okay," Mrs. Brewer said. "We've only just gotten it renovated and actually still have a bit more to do, but we're happy to have people come in and visit."

"I'll have to make it a point to do that soon," Joanna said. "What can I do for you?"

"Well, I'm sorry to bother you, but I heard you were investigating a possible haunting at the library."

Oh, no, Joanna thought. Here we go again with another person upset about 'defacing' the building.

"Before you go any further," Joanna said, her tone decidedly cooler. "We are not doing anything to destroy or deface the building as someone may have told you, Mrs. Brewer."

"No, it's not that at all," Mrs. Brewer said. "And please call me Gert."

"Okay, Gert," Joanna replied. "Then why are you here?"

"It's kind of a delicate situation," she said. "May I sit with you for a few moments while I explain?"

"Sure," Joanna said, stepping aside so the woman could sit on the top step as Joanna was when she arrived. "Can I get you a cup of coffee or anything?"

"No, I'm okay," she said, taking a dainty seat on the porch and waiting for Joanna to do the same. Gert took a breath as if preparing herself or finding the right words. "I don't know how to say this, so I'll just plough forward. You stop me if you have any questions."

"Fair enough," Joanna said taking a sip of her coffee and waiting for whatever was coming next.

"I've been on the board of the Savin House for years now, since the beginning when someone decided to save it from the wrecking ball." She paused. "It is a beautiful old house from the early 1800's with the land parcel there even before then when this wasn't even West Haven yet."

"I've read a lot of history of this town due to this investigation," Joanna said.

"I'm sure you have," Gert said. "I'm a fan of your novels and appreciate the detail that goes into writing them."

"Thank you very much," Joanna said, wondering where this was all heading. As if reading Joanna's mind, Gert continued.

"I'm sure you're wondering what a house has to do with the investigation, but it has a lot to do with it in fact. The house was first owned by another family. The Adamsons were the original owners of the house, but one of the owners sold it to the Savin family around the time the new library was built at the turn of the 20th century, around 1900 or so."

"Ron Adamson's family owned it way back when?" Joanna said. The story was getting more interesting and she waited for Gert to say more.

"Yes, and I understand he is pushing to stop your investigation," Gert said.

"He is, but how do you know?"

"This may be a city, but it's a small town at heart," she smiled. "Everyone knows everything about everybody if you've lived here long enough."

"Don't I know it!" Joanna grinned. "So what does this house have to do with anything?"

"We, all of us on the Board of Directors of the Savin House, think both the Savin and the old building that was there before the library was first built were depots on the Underground Railroad."

"Yes, I know about the library and it's not surprising that house may have been, but I still don't see the connection." Joanna couldn't imagine Gert or anyone at the Savin House knew of the murder, but she was soon to learn she was wrong.

"We have information from old records we've found that the Adamson owner, the one who sold the home to the Savins, may have murdered two of his workers and buried them in the old root cellar by the kitchen door of the first house." Gert waited. "You don't seem surprised."

"I'm not, though I figured the root cellar I had heard about was at the house in which he lived," Joanna said, wondering how much she should divulge to this woman she had just met. "I can't tell you how I know, but I know for a fact Ron Adamson's ancestor had two of his workers murdered." Joanna now paused before continuing. "May I count on your discretion? I don't want to say anything about one's family and have people start talking about that."

"Oh, you have the utmost discretion from me," Gert said. "I have had to keep an untold number of secrets as a law clerk for many years. I'm retired now, but I am in the habit of keeping secrets for everyone!"

Joanna continued.

"Mr. Adamson's relative had two of his household workers, two men, murdered when they threatened to tell the authorities they were not being paid. They were essentially slaves even after slavery had officially ended."

"Do you think that's the reason Adamson is trying to stop your investigation at the library?" Gert asked. "It was so many years ago, but Ron is always worried about what people think of him even though he is a grouchy guy."

"I think that is exactly the reason," Joanna said. Now she had a feeling she knew why she had been directed to dig up that root cellar. She got more excited about the meeting with the guy who worked the metal detector.

"Have you spoken to him about this?" Gert asked. "I am not sure he would admit it."

"I'm waiting to have more concrete evidence before I speak to him," Joanna said. "We may have discovered something that could prove the murder story, but I don't want to say much until we are certain."

"That's interesting," Gert said, her eyes lighting up at the information. "I didn't know you had any idea about the murders. I just thought you were investigating sounds in the old part of the library."

"It began that way, but now it's something else entirely, or I should say it is sounds and more," Joanna said.

"Well, good," Gert said, standing up and walking down the steps to the front sidewalk. "I didn't want to interrupt your workday, but I felt you needed to know this information."

"Thank you, Gert," Joanna said. "I appreciate your candor. This information adds to the pile of evidence I already have."

"It sounds like something you can write in one of your books!" Gert said, smiling and clasping her hands.

"It does, doesn't it?" Joanna grinned. "We'll see. For now, I just want to figure out where these noises are coming from and who murdered whom, if a murder occurred at all. It seems it did."

"It certainly does," Gert said, turning on her heel to leave. "Okay, I won't keep you. It was nice meeting you today."

"You as well!" Joanna said. "And thank you for the information. I do appreciate it and won't tell a soul other than one of my friends who is part of my investigating team, I think you would call it."

"All right, then," Gert said. "Have a good day and good luck!"

"Thank you," Joanna said. She watched Gert drive away and considered what she said. If the house was another depot, perhaps the Adamson ancestor found out about it which led to his murdering these two men or having them murdered which was the same thing.

Joanna couldn't wait to tell Anne this interesting piece of information.

CHAPTER 18

Joanna showed up at the library at exactly 8:15 Monday night. Sal's detectorist had no problem meeting them there and it seemed everyone else, and a few others, were waiting at the library already. Joanna was glad she had called Anne to fill her in ahead of time. There would be no way to get her alone tonight.

"Who are all these people?" Joanna asked Anne when she reached her.

"I think your detector guy told them what he was doing," Anne frowned. "I guess Sal didn't fill him in on the 'confidentiality' part of this whole thing."

"Yikes," Joanna muttered. "We're never going to be able to keep this quiet now."

"Nope," Anne replied. At that moment, Buddy Lawson arrived.

"Who are all these people?" he asked, parroting Joanna's question without knowing it. Just then Sal walked up to the trio.

"I am so sorry," he addressed Joanna. "I told him to keep it to himself, but he must have told somebody."

"Obviously," Anne said. "It's not your fault, though."

"Yeah, Sal," Joanna added. "I appreciate your finding someone to do this. We'll just deal with the commotion as best we can."

"I know you didn't want the whole city to know we were doing this," he said. "I'm going to have a talk with him." Sal started walking over to Billy, the detectorist as he arrived.

"No, don't worry about it, Sal," Joanna said. "I don't want him to feel bad."

"Yes, people were bound to get wind of this at some point," Lawson said. "It just happened to be now."

"I'm surprised it took this long," Anne said, and Buddy nodded.

"I was about to say the same thing," he said. At that moment, Celine came to the door to let them in.

"What is this?" she asked Joanna and Anne. "I'd rather not have all of these people here after hours."

"I agree," Lawson said and addressed the small crowd of people who came to gawk. "Everyone, we can't have you all coming into the library after hours," he said. "I apologize, but this is not a public event. We will have more information for you soon, but for now, I am only allowing the few of us involved in this investigation to be here."

The crowd let out a collective groan but began to walk to their cars or down Campbell Avenue for a quick beer with their friends before going home. The investigating group went in with the detectorist in front and Sal behind him giving him a dirty look behind his back. Joanna suspected he had spoken to him already and heard him apologize to Celine as he passed her on his way into the building.

Laura, Nick and Sylvia appeared through the crowd.

"I let them come tonight, Celine," Joanna said. "If you remember, they're from our Saturday group. They want to help. I hope that's okay."

"Sure," Celine said. She locked the front door behind everyone, and then led the way into the Reference Room. By the time Joanna got in, Sal had already removed the tapestry and opened the door.

Luke, the detectorist, peered inside.

"Are there any lights in here?" he asked.

"No," Sal replied, "but I have a work light I'm plugging in now. Give me your detector and I'll plug that in, too." He had taken his work light into the building with him and was looking for an outlet as Luke spoke. "There. I'll take you in so I can show you where Joanna wants you to look."

Sal walked without fear, though Joanna suspected there was more than a little fear involved and he was all show.

"It's about three feet in, right Joanna?" he asked as he walked forward with Luke behind him.

"Yes," Joanna replied. "It's right about where you're standing now."

Sal nodded, then stepped farther in while shining the light so Luke could see. Luke turned on his detector and swept it back and forth over the area indicated. There must have been nails in the door to the cellar because the detector immediately started beeping.

"Does that mean there's a lot or a little metal there?" Lawson asked.

"It means a nail or some type of metal is right below my detector," Luke said. "It makes less noise when I move to the side. Hold on a minute." Luke moved the detector back, forth, up and down before continuing. "It seems to be a square of metal, like the door you were looking for."

"Wait a minute," Sal said. "Can someone hand in a screwdriver from my tool box? Look for one with a flat head."

Joanna went over to the toolbox and did as he asked. Sal then confirmed with Luke where the border of the door should be and drew a box in the dirt.

"Let's go through the rest of this just in case there is anything else," he said whereby he and Luke did just that.

"I don't see anything else under here," Luke said, turning off his detector and walking out of the room with Sal behind him.

"So what happens now?" Celine asked.

"My suggestion is to get someone in there to dig into the floor where we think the door to the cellar is," Sal said.

"Can you do that or do we have to get someone else in here?" Joanna asked.

"I can do it if it doesn't violate any rules," Sal said. "I would just have to come back with a shovel and some other things, then Luke would have to go over whatever we find inside."

"I don't think it will violate any rules," Lawson said. "The Board has already given its permission to dig if necessary."

"Well, then, just give me a minute while I run out to my truck," Sal said. "Luke, drop that and come with me."

"No problem," Luke said, laying the metal detector on the floor just outside the door and following Sal.

Celine went to unlock the door for them while the others waited. When they returned, Sal had three shovels with him.

"If it's okay with you, we can see if we can reach the door right now," Sal said. "Luke can help."

"That's fine," Lawson replied. "As I said, I've already gotten permission to dig just in case we found something. Let's see how far you get tonight."

With that, Sal laid the work light on the floor just past the marked area and the two men started digging.

"This is exciting!" Anne said. "It's a real excavation, isn't it?"

"It is," Joanna said. "I don't like thinking about what we might find when we get the door open, though."

"I agree," Lawson said as he watched the activities in the closet.

The two men dug for about thirty minutes while the others waited around for them to finish. Joanna was checking email on her phone when Sal alerted her.

"That's it," he said. "We have a cellar door."

Sal and Luke came out of the room to let Joanna, Anne, Buddy Lawson and Celine go in one at a time. They each peered on the dirt-dusted square that served as a door to a root cellar in an earlier life.

Anne turned to Joanna. "So, what do you think we should do now? Are you getting any vibes or anything?"

"I am," Joanna said, cocking her head to the side and closing her eyes. "The souls are very active as if they are swirling around with excitement." She opened her eyes and looked at Anne. "We're doing the right thing."

"That's just fascinating," Lawson said. "How do you know what they're saying?" And then he caught himself. "Never mind. That would require more time than we have right now with all of the questions I want to ask you."

"Should we open the door now?" Sal asked. "Would you prefer to leave it as it is and come back another night? It's already 9:30, but I'm happy to stay," he said as he looked at his watch.

Joanna looked at the others and hoped she was reading the room correctly.

"I'd like to stay if that works for you, Sal," she said. She was grateful when the others erupted with enthusiasm.

"Of course I want to stay, but I have no problem if anyone else leaves," Lawson said.

"No, way," Anne said. "This is exciting!"

"I agree," Celine said.

Sal looked at Luke who nodded. "I'm ready," he said and headed back into the closet with Sal and a crowbar. The two men carefully punched into the border of the trap door until they could easily lift it with the end of Sal's crowbar and the shovel Luke had been using.

Joanna thought it was like an Egyptian excavation like opening a tomb, and then realized that's exactly what it was. There was a distinct possibility that Luke's metal detector was going to find more metal, this time buttons to a shirt or nails in a boot. The problem was these would belong to two dead men if the journal and Adamson's nephew were correct and Joanna had no reason to believe otherwise.

Sal set aside the crowbar after gently lifting the edge of the door, then inserted his hand under the edge.

"Are you ready for this?" Sal asked Joanna who had stationed herself just inside the doorway to the room.

"I think so," she said, uncertainty coloring her response. "Go ahead."

The two men lifted the old door to the root cellar and laid it down. They stood back while Sal got the light that was still lying a few inches away and then lifted it up to illuminate the hole.

What they saw was indeed a cellar. The cavernous space went down about three feet with a steps leading down into a space whose size was impossible to ascertain. The men looked down into the hole, then quickly up at Joanna.

"Honestly, if there's a body in there, I don't want to go anywhere near it," Sal said while Luke backed away in agreement.

"I don't think we should go in there tonight," Lawson said looking over Joanna's shoulder. "We should have a police officer or a detective in here with us when anyone goes down there."

"Yes, of course," Joanna said. "We don't want to disturb the evidence if there is something, or someone, down there."

"It also may not be safe," Sal added.

"Okay, Sal, close it up, please," Lawson asked. "Celine, do you have another tapestry or a cheap rug we could put over the door for now?"

"Wait," Joanna said and went out into the other room for a moment. She came back with the towel she had used previously to sit on when she was listening to the souls inside this room. "Use this."

Sal took the towel and spread it over the door with Luke's help while he held the work light.

"Okay, let's get out of here," Joanna said. "Buddy, will you call the police tomorrow morning and let me know when they're coming in here?"

"I would imagine they would want to come in right away," he said. "The only problem with that is keeping this discovery from the public."

"I think that's a dream at this point," Anne said. "They've already gotten wind of our investigation. If they see the police here, they're going to be even more curious. Besides, it's a public building. The cops can only keep them back during business hours, right?"

"Maybe they can close the Reference Room while they're in here investigating," Celine said. "We've done it for short periods when we've had work done like when we had to patch the ceiling after hurricane damage caused it to leak."

"That's true," Lawson said. "Okay, we'll do that tomorrow while the police are in here."

"Please keep me updated," Joanna said as she grabbed her bag. Sal had already closed the outer door, covered it and he and Luke had gathered their equipment. "I want to be here when they go into that room."

"You'll probably have to be here," Lawson said. "They might have some questions for you."

"That's true," Joanna said.

"I'm so sorry I got you involved in all of this," Celine said, flipping off the lights and following the group out into the hallway. "If it weren't for me, you would not be here."

"I don't regret it at all," Joanna said. "First, I was happy to help you, but now it's become an obsession. I need to know what happened here and how it happened, not to mention putting the souls to rest."

"Thank you," Celine said, laying a hand on Joanna's forearm. "I really appreciate it."

"No problem Celine," Joanna said, briefly laying her own hand over Celine's.

"Okay, folks," Lawson said, pushing the inner door open. "I'll call the police, then call Joanna and Celine with the details. If they need you, Sal, can you be here, too?"

"No problem, Buddy," he said. "My current client won't mind too much." He smirked.

"Uh, that would be me," Joanna chuckled. "Thanks, Sal and thank you, too, Luke."

"Don't worry about it," Sal said.

"My pleasure," seconded Luke. "I'm here if you need me to come back."

"Thank you again," Joanna said and pushed through the outer door that Celine had just unlocked. Joanna was grateful none of the bystanders were around. She hadn't wanted to be right, in all honesty. There were probably two men down in that root cellar whose only wish was to be paid and they were murdered instead.

Joanna shook her head.

"I'll see you soon," she said to no one in particular and got into her car for the short drive home. She didn't even know these men and her heart broke for them. From what she had read in the journal, they were probably only in their mid-thirties. Life was ahead of them and it was cruelly snuffed by a greedy employer. 'Not even an employer, but a slave owner from what it sounded like. The unfairness of it all saddened Joanna. She would put the sadness aside for now and wait until the conclusion of this chapter tomorrow.

The next morning, Joanna knew she needed to talk to Ron Adamson urgently. He had no idea the police were going to look at the root cellar, and discover the evidence of his family's crime, and Joanna felt it the right thing to do was to inform him.

Instead of calling and being rebuffed, she decided to go over to his house. It would be much more difficult for him to be nasty to her in person. At least that was what she hoped.

Adamson lived in one of those beautiful houses facing the water on Ocean Avenue. Joanna envied people who got to live in these houses for she had always wanted to live in one. She loved the sound of the waves hitting the shore and the whooshing sound the water made when the tide came in. She remembered as a child being far out on the sand during dead low tide, smacking the mud with her bare feet trying to get the little clams to spit. When the tide started coming in, you could hear it in the distance and knew it was time to head back to shore.

Joanna pulled into the side street next to Adamson's house. He must have been looking out of his window because he was standing in his open front door by the time Joanna got out of her car and was walking up the front walkway.

"This can't be good," he said when he saw her. "And how did you find out where I live?"

"You should worry about what's online if you don't want visitors," Joanna said. "I did a quick online search and found your public information almost immediately."

"Well, I'll look into that because I definitely don't want visitors," he replied. They stared one another down before Adamson chose to be gracious. "Now that you're here, would you like to come in?"

"I would love to," Joanna said, finishing her walk up the stairs and stepping into his front hall. "I won't be here too long, so don't worry."

"Okay, but I need more coffee and just brewed a fresh pot. Would you like some?" he offered. It smelled Heavenly to Joanna, so she accepted. While he went to pour her a cup, she glanced at an incoming text – it was time to schedule an oil change - and then walked around his front room. It was homey as if he had lived there quite a while. Adamson returned, so she asked him when he moved in, just to break the ice. He wasn't going to like what she was going to say, so why not warm him up a bit?

"This is my family's home, or it has been for a generation at least," he said, probably thinking about that errant ancestor of his. "My grandfather bought this house soon after my father was born. That was sometime in the mid-forties."

"It's cozy and looks well-loved," she responded. The coffee really was good.

"I'm sure you didn't come here to talk about my house," he said, taking a sip from his own cup.

"You're right," Joanna said. "And you're not going to like any of it, honestly."

"I already don't like what you're doing," he responded. "How could it get worse?"

And then she told him about what she had learned. He paled as Joanna laid out his great-grandfather's crime, what they found in the closed-off closet, and what was happening that morning.

"Why would you think my great-grandfather…" he blustered.

"Because I read the journal," she said, her stomach sinking as she said it.

Adamson placed his cup on the coffee table with a jolt as his head swiveled toward his bookcase. He stood up, following where his eyes sought out the old notebook. It wasn't there, of course, and his head snapped back to take in Joanna as if she was from another planet.

"Did you break into my house?" he boomed theatrically. "Or did you have someone do it for you? How dare you!"

"Of course I didn't break into your house," she retorted. "Someone who had access to it gave it to me to look at."

"Who? Who would do that?" he asked, coming back to his chair and leaning forward. "The only person who has been here has been..." And then the reality sunk in. "Daniel gave it to you? But why?"

"He wanted to make sure the truth was told," she said, sipping her coffee in case she was kicked out soon. It really was good!

"Why would he want that truth out there? I certainly don't," he said, sitting back in his chair, cupping his mug as if it held some security, like a teddy bear or a security blanket.

"But it was years ago, Ron," Joanna said. "There is no shame on you if your ancestor did something sinister over a hundred years ago."

"Yes. It is shameful and reflects badly on my entire family," he said, reserved now as he spoke. "I don't see why Daniel doesn't feel that way. Besides, where is my journal? I want it

back ... now."

"I don't have it," Joanna lied. It was in her purse, but she didn't want him to destroy the evidence if it was needed. "I don't know if it may be used as evidence, so it's safe with someone else." Again, a lie, but he didn't have to know that.

"Evidence?" he croaked. "You said yourself the crime was over a hundred years ago."

"Yes, but the police still have to investigate what we found," she replied, and then told Adamson about the root cellar's opening the night before.

"The police?" he shouted. "Why would the police care? Are they coming here?" He looked over his shoulder out the window as if two officers might suddenly materialize.

"No, not here, but they will be at the library this morning," Joanna said, placing her almost-empty mug on the table before her and standing. "In fact, they should be there in about a half an hour. I got a text while you were in the kitchen."

"I don't understand why you have to wreck a person's character just for fun," he said, his eyes flaming.

"We are not wrecking anything, Ron, just getting to the truth," Joanna responded.

"Do you really expect anyone to believe someone heard a story from a ghost and then investigated it? That's preposterous," he said.

"But it's not because it was all written down in your great-grandfather's journal," Joanna said. "And it honestly does not ruin your character even if it's something your relative did generations ago. I'm not sure why you don't see that or why you're so paranoid."

"This is not happening if I have anything to do with it," Adamson blustered.

"Well, I hate to tell you, but it already has," Joanna said. "The police will be there this morning." She reached for her purse from the floor next to the chair. "I'll meet you there?" she asked, correctly expecting he would want to be there.

"I'm right behind you," he said, grabbing both mugs and walking to the kitchen to put them in the sink. "You can show yourself out," he threw over his shoulder as he went.

Joanna did just that and drove to the library.

CHAPTER 19

When Joanna pulled up to the library, there was a detective parked in front on the street. She hoped it wouldn't draw attention to the investigation, but of course she was wrong. When she walked in just a little after ten in the morning, she found a plainclothes police officer just outside the doors of the Reference Room, holding back a small crowd. The volume of the chatter rose slightly when the people saw her and she mumbled greetings as she walked through the door the officer opened for her. Of course he knew who she was after her minor celebrity status brought on by the Sophia situation.

"Hello, everyone," she said as she came into the room. There she found Celine, Anne, Buddy Lawson and the two contractors. Sal had already been into the empty room to open the door for the detectives and remained standing at the top of the hole in the floor, holding the work light low inside so they could see.

Joanna saw Sal hand in the light to a detective who was inside the apparently small space. It looked to Joanna as if he had found something if he wanted the light. She asked Anne.

"Did he find anything yet?" Joanna asked.

"It looks as if he's finding something just now, doesn't it?" she parroted Joanna's thoughts as she leaned toward the doorway to listen better.

Suddenly there was a commotion in the hallway and the group turned toward it.

"Is it okay if this man comes in?" the officer at the door asked Lawson. At that point Adamson pushed past the police officer.

"Of course it is," he said and Lawson nodded to the police officer who returned to his post outside the doors. "Did they find anything?"

"We're still waiting," Joanna said garnering surreptitious glances from Celine and Anne. Joanna put up a hand motioning that she would explain later. For now, they all just stood waiting.

"We found something," the detective called out from inside the hole. He handed the work light to Sal who helped him out. Sal then reached in and helped out a second person, Joanna assumed it was another detective. They both came out of the room brushing off dirt with Sal following.

The first detective out of the hole confirmed their suspicions.

"Well, we definitely found a body, maybe two, but I ask you not to tell anyone outside this room," he warned. "We're going to get another metal detector person in here."

Everyone's head whipped toward Luke and he looked back.

"No offense," said the detective. "We need an official person for an official investigation."

"I have no problem with that," he said.

"I think we all understand," Joanna said. "May I have your names?"

"Oh, I'm sorry," the first detective who spoke apologized. "I'm Detective Corradino and this is Detective Fantarella." They both put out their hands to shake Joanna's before Joanna dug out her notebook to write down both names for her own records and they shook hands with each member of the assembled group. They were both of average height wearing the typical detective uniform of trousers, shirt and tie and a sports jacket, which they had tossed on one of the tables; shoes polished and badges clipped to their belt buckles.

"I know who you are," said the second detective, Fantarella, as he offered his hand to Joanna to shake.

"That's flattering," she said. "Do you read my books?"

"I do and so does my wife," he said, a bit star struck. "We heard you read at an event a few years ago. Very interesting."

"Thank you," Joanna said again. "So when do you think you can get the detectorist in here?"

"Oh, we've already called him," Detective Corradino said. "He should be here in a couple of minutes."

Just as he finished his sentence, a man with a metal detector came into the room. He was short with dark, curly hair, and loaded up with equipment including what looked like a metal detector.

"I'm here," he said to the group. "What am I looking at?"

"You're all business, aren't you?" Anne said with a grin.

"I'm sorry," he said realizing how gruff he had been. "I have several assignments to get to and squeezed this one in since it was just down the street from the Police Station. I don't often do this, so it is strange to have so many sites to visit. I bunched them all into one day." He put down his gear and looked around for the person in charge. "I'm Detective Simmons," he said, settling on Anne first, then Lawson and Joanna. "And I know you already," he said to Celine. "My kids are in here all the time; Maddie and Michael."

"Oh, I know them, I think," Celine said. "They're such well-behaved kids with a definite thirst for knowledge."

The detective got right down to business.

"I understand you've already had someone work on this with a detector," he said, looking at Luke who stood next to his equipment.

"That was me, but I only used it to find the door," he said. "I didn't go in. We waited for you detectives to do that."

"And that's why we grabbed you before you moved on for the day," Detective Corradino interjected. "Joe and I went down there today," he said, indicating the room and leading Simmons over. "We were looking for two bodies and I think we found them."

Simmons looked around at the faces before him.

"I can tell there's more to the story, but I'll have to read the report when I have time," he said, moving into the room. "Let me just get down there and see what we've got."

"This is absolutely ridiculous," Adamson said. "There is no need for any of this!"

"Yes, there is if there is a body down there," Detective Fantarella said. "It doesn't matter how old it is, it's someone's life that was snuffed out."

"Am I going to be arrested for this?" Adamson asked. "I did nothing except keep quiet about what I read in a journal."

"Of course not," Detective Corradino said. "We just need to get to the bottom of this and, hopefully, give the two people down there a dignified burial. We'll decide all of that later. Right now, we just need to confirm what we have here."

Sal and Luke went into the room and opened the door to the root cellar, carefully and slowly so they did not damage the wood.

"Here, let me climb down and you can hand it to me," he said to Sal, giving him the metal detecting equipment. "Do you have any light?"

"Yes," Luke said, turning on the work light and lowering it down after Sal handed down Detective Simmons' equipment. The two stood back as the other two detectives crammed into the small room.

"Look toward the back there," Corradino said as the metal detector started beeping slowly. "Toward Campbell Avenue."

"I think I see a bag," Simmons said. "What am I looking for, nails like in a shoe?"

"Yes," responded Detective Fantarella. "That and buttons on a jacket."

Detective Simmons went farther into the cellar as directed by the other two detectives and his metal detector immediately started beeping more urgently.

"I'm coming on something here," said the voice from the cellar. The beeping got faster and faster as if there was one beep. "I got it."

The four men in the room looked at each other as did the group in the outer room.

"I'm afraid to know what it is," Joanna said.

"Me, too," Anne said, reaching over and taking Joanna's arm for comfort.

A few more moments passed as Detective Simmons went over the area he found and then turned off his metal detector. The next sound those in the closet could hear were the clicks of his cell phone as he took pictures.

"I'm not going to ask if you found anything because we could hear all of the beeping, but do you know what you found?" Detective Fantarella asked as they helped Detective Simmons out of the root cellar with all of his equipment, holding Sal's work light.

"Yes," Detective Simmons said. "We have two bodies down there."

Joanna heard Adamson draw in a quick breath.

"How do you know?" Joanna asked. "I mean I don't doubt you, but I'm just curious how you know it's two bodies."

"Well," he said, wiping off his pants and coming out into the main room. "I located two sets of shoe buttons, metal, and a few buttons where two jackets would be."

"Oh my God," Anne said. "There have been two bodies in here all these years?"

"It looks like it," Detective Simmons said.

She glanced at Adamson who stared defiantly back at her.

"Are there any others?" asked Buddy Lawson.

"Not that I can tell," said Detective Simmons. "I did a sweep of the whole room and those two were the only bodies I found. There were a few metal plates, probably, and maybe a few lids to those glass canning jars people used to can with, but no other bodies."

"What did it look like?" asked Detective Fantarella. "I mean, do we have skeletons or bodies?"

"Definitely only partial skeletons at this point," Detective Simmons responded. "We have a couple of buttons from their clothing, nails from their shoes, but other than that, just skeletons."

Detectives Corradino and Fantarella exchanged glances before ending the exchange.

"Okay, Mark," Corradino said, putting out his hand to shake. "I appreciate your squeezing us into your schedule."

"No problem, Jim," he said, shaking his hand and then taking his equipment from Luke. "I appreciate you calling me. This is going to be interesting. Make sure you send me the report when you're finished writing it."

"We will," Fantarella said. With that, Detective Simmons walked out of the Reference Room leaving a quiet group in his wake.

"Wow," Lawson said. "I know we expected that, but it's difficult to hear it."

"You all realize we're going to need statements from each of you, don't you?" Detective Corradino said. "I mean Buddy told me what was going on, and none of you are suspects in any way, but I definitely need to take statements for my report."

The group tried not to look at Adamson. Though he was not involved either, he kept this information from the authorities for presumably many years depending on when he read it in the journal.

Joanna wondered if he could get in trouble for omitting the information his great grandfather detailed in his journal. As if he knew they were all thinking about him, Ron Adamson spoke.

"I know you're all wondering why I never said anything about this," he said.

"Actually, I was," Anne said. "I can't speak for anyone else."

He looked at Joanna and then began to explain.

"I am on the Library Board and do a lot for this city," he began. "I found out about this years ago when my house was left to me and I found the journal but I didn't want to tarnish my family's name by saying anything."

"But it wasn't you who did this," Celine said.

"I know that, but it was my family," he said as if speaking to a child.

"I'm just glad you called us," Detective Corradino said to Lawson. "We'll get someone here to dig them up to confirm they are bodies and to bury them. Maybe we'll be able to identify them, too."

"What do you think the library will do with the room?" Anne asked.

"That's up to the Board," Lawson said. "I'll inform them today and we'll decide. For now, if you fellas are finished, we can have Sal close everything up and replace the tapestry."

"Yes, do that, but we're going to have make this a crime scene for now and close up the Reference Room, at least for today," Detective Fantarella said. "I'll grab the tape from the car."

While he went out to get the crime scene tape, Sal and Luke removed Joanna's blanket, closed the cellar door as well as the entry, and replaced the tapestry. By this time, Detective Fantarella had returned.

"There are a still a few people out there, but I told them the room would be closed for the day," he said, reaching for a chair and tying the tape between that one and another Detective Corradino had pulled out.

"I guess you get an unexpected day off, Celine," Lawson said.

"Oh, don't worry about me," she said. "There's always tons to do in a library believe it or not. It is okay if I stay in the room, isn't it?" she asked the detectives.

"No, I'm sorry, but you're going to have to leave until we open the room up again," Detective Corradino said. "We'll have an officer stationed outside the door here, but you'll have to work outside the Reference Room for today. I'm sorry."

"No problem," Celine said, already walking over to her desk and removing a notebook and paperwork that would carry her through the day. "If I finish my paperwork, I can always help reshelve returned books or maybe I'll go work in the Children's Library for today."

"That sounds nice," Anne said. "I love reading to the children when I can."

"Well, come with me and we can see when they may need someone for a story time," Celine said. "Are we finished here?" she asked the detectives, her arms full of notebooks and papers.

"I think you're good," Detective Fantarella said. "We're keeping this uniformed officer to guard the room until the diggers are finished. We'll close it all up and let you know when the room is reopened after that."

"Okay," she replied. "I appreciate it if you make sure they are careful when they come in. I'd rather not have dirt all over the floor if at all possible."

"No problem," Detective Corradino said. "I'll make sure the officer keeps tabs on whoever is going to remove the bodies. We'll get a book lover in here. I promise."

"Thank you," Celine said. "And you can find me upstairs if you need me for a statement or if you have any more questions." With that, she turned to Anne. "Are you ready to leave, Anne?"

"I'm ready," Anne said. "I'll talk to you later, Joanna." With that she was off to see if she could read to the 'littles.'

"I'm leaving, too," Adamson said.

"We need your statement," Detective Fantarella said. "Give me your number and we can either stop by your house or you can come down to the station within the next couple of days."

Ron Adamson grumbled but complied.

"I would rather not have a squad car at my house," Adamson said. "It would look like I did something."

"We use the unmarked vehicles," Detective Fantarella said. "Don't worry about it. Besides, you know this city. Everyone will know the whole story by tonight or they'll make one up."

"I get it," Adamson said. He turned on his heel and left the Reference Room. Some curious onlookers recognized him and the little bunch left at the door buzzed with speculation. The detective was right about the entire city knowing what happened by tonight.

"Do you need me to stay, Detective?" Joanna addressed both men.

"If you have a moment to give me a statement, that would be helpful," Detective Corradino answered. "We can sit over at one of the tables here. And Mr. Lawson, if you could join us, I could take your statement, too."

"No problem, Detective," he said, following Joanna and Detective Corradino over to a table at the back of the room.

"Is it okay if Luke and I take off?" Joanna heard Sal ask Detective Fantarella.

"Sure," he said. "I know you have work to do. We'll get your number from Ms. Davis and find out when you can come in for your statement, and yours, too," he said, indicating Luke standing by.

"No problem," Sal said.

"Thanks for the help, both of you," Detective Corradino shouted from the other side of the room where he sat. "So, tell me the story of how we got here. Start at the beginning and don't leave anything out."

Joanna began filling the detective in on the details with Lawson adding his part of the story here and there. Joanna was happy to see the detective did not flinch when she spoke about dead people hanging around and speaking to her. He knew about the Sophia case and was another true believer.

"Where is the journal now?" he asked when she finished telling him about her meeting with Daniel, Adamson's nephew.

"It's in my purse," she said, digging it out and handing it over. She had already made copies of the pages that interested her, but she kept that information to herself.

Detective Corradino flipped through the notebook briefly and then showed it to Detective Fantarella before pulling a sticky note from his bag and marking it as evidence, presumably to bag it more formally when they finished here.

"Is Mr. Adamson going to be charged with anything?" Joanna asked.

"No," both detectives said at once. "This happened long ago," Detective Corradino said. "We just have to make sure the bodies are identified, if possible, and buried with respect."

"Where do you think they'll be buried?" Lawson asked.

"We have space in various cemeteries in Connecticut," Detective Fantarella said as Detective Corradino jotted down a few notes. "We may even be able to figure out the names of these two guys, assuming they are men."

"Yes, they were two servants in the old Mr. Adamson's house and they sometimes helped on his tobacco farm," Joanna said. "I stuck a sticky note in the journal where that part began."

"I gotta ask," Detective Fantarella said, sitting at the table on the other side of the table. "Did you see them when they spoke to you? How does that work?"

Joanna inwardly groaned as she thought about having to explain this to the well-meaning detective. He was just interested, Joanna knew. She really should come up with an easy way to explain all of this, like an elevator speech.

"I can sometimes see them and hear them, but it's more like getting a sense of what they want to convey. I also may 'see' them in another sense if that makes sense?" she answered.

"Oh, it makes sense to me," Detective Fantarella said. "I had a grandmother who had the gift. Her dead grandmother used to appear to her when anything major was going to happen to the family. Kind of like a warning."

"That's exactly the kind of thing that happens to me," Joanna said. "If you really want to know, we can grab a coffee sometime or I can come into the station to explain it."

"That would be interesting," he said. "Detective Sosa tried to explain it to me once, but it was difficult to wrap my head around it all."

"He was a great help to me with that other case," Joanna said. "He's asked me to be available should he need me for other cases."

"Yes," Detective Corradino added. "You are on our list of 'psychics' or 'mediums' should we need someone."

"I'm happy to help if I can," Joanna replied. "Even though I'm pretty new to all of it."

"So, what happens now?" Lawson asked. "You said someone is going to come today to dig out the bodies. What then?"

"The funeral home will clean up the bodies and their clothing as best as possible, and then the city will probably have some sort of service for them," Detective Corradino said. "They usually put John Does in various cemeteries around the state that have space for unknown or homeless people. They'll go in one of those."

"I'd like to know when the service will be so I can attend," Joanna said.

"Me too," added Lawson. "In fact, I can help make the arrangements if you put me in touch with the undertaker."

"Will do," replied Detective Corradino.

Shortly after this, the police officer who had been guarding the door stepped inside and shut the door behind him.

"Detectives?" he said. "I just got orders that the next shift will send someone to replace me."

"Perfect," Detective Fantarella said. "Thank you. We'll be out of here shortly."

"No problem," the officer said and resumed his place outside the Reference Room for a few minutes, waiting for the next shift.

"Is there anything else you can tell me that you think might be relevant to this situation?" Detective Corradino asked. "It may be a tiny detail to you, but it may end up meaning something to us."

Joanna scoured her mind for a moment and then thought of the little boy.

"There was a little boy who spoke to me at first," she said, knowing they were both believers. "He apparently lost his mother while they were fleeing north on the Underground Railroad."

"Is his body there, too?" Detective Fantarella asked.

"No, there are no other bodies there," she responded.

"Then it's probably not relevant, but it's definitely interesting!" Detective Corradino said, scribbling the information in his notebook anyway.

The two detectives looked at each other and then Detective Corradino spoke.

"Okay, I guess that's it for now," he said. "We shouldn't have to bother you again with any questions, but we'll be in touch if we think of anything else."

"Thank you, detectives," Joanna said, rising from her chair and reaching out to shake each detective's hand. Buddy Lawson did the same.

"So, do you do this type of investigation often?" Detective Fantarella asked. "It's interesting stuff!"

"No, this is only the second time and only because Celine, the librarian, could not figure out where the noises were coming from."

"Didn't you say Sosa put you on a list of psychics the department can call if we need them?" Detective Corradino asked.

"He did, but he hasn't called me yet," Joanna responded. They all stopped talking as they got to the door of the Reference Room. Joanna didn't want anyone who was waiting outside the room to hear their discussion and the others with her didn't seem to want that either. She found it funny that none of those people said anything, though, to her or the detectives with her. They just stood there watching them all leave like a red carpet even for a movie premiere.

She noticed the librarians at the desk looked up, too, but they just waved before returning to their duties at the desk.

Joanna exchanged pleasantries with the three men before getting in her car and driving away. She wondered if she should drive over to Adamson's house and … what? Apologize? For some reason he was upset that his family was outed, but Joanna still didn't understand why. It happened generations ago. His only knowledge of it was by way of a journal his great-grandfather kept.

Her car made its way to his house. Whether she would be welcome remained to be seen, but she thought she would find a way to mend fences. She had no idea why she felt that way. Ron Adamson had been nothing but rude for the most part, but for some reason, she wanted to clear the air with him.

Joanna got out of the car and found Adamson already standing in his doorway, the look on his face inscrutable.

"Hello," she started. "May I come in for a moment?"

He blinked and opened the door wide for her to pass, indicating she should go into the front room when she got inside. The tension was thick.

"May I sit down?" she asked.

"Yes, of course," he replied. "Would you like some coffee or something else to drink?"

"No, thanks," she said. "I just wanted to have a little chat."

"What about? You are about to let the whole town know a secret that has been well-kept for years."

"It actually wasn't me who did that," she said.

"Oh, yes, I know. It was a ghost who told you things," he waved away her explanation. "I've already heard the librarian heard noises, but it remains that the world will know what my great-grandfather did."

"But that's not you, Ron," she said, hoping the use of his first name might warm him up a little. "It was your ancestor, not you. Since then, your father and then you have done a lot for the people of this city. I guarantee they are not going to hold this against you."

"You don't know that," he said. He was leaning forward with his arms resting on his lap, staring at the old rug. He looked so dejected that Joanna felt sorry for him.

"I know if you hold your head up high, no one will think any less of you," Joanna said.

"Where is my journal?" he asked taking his eyes from the floor suddenly. "Did you have to give it to the police?"

"I did, but you'll get it back soon, I think," she said, and then she explained what was probably going to happen in the next few days. "The Medical Examiner was heading to the library when I left. As I understand it, they will see if they can find out how they died, but in this case, I don't think there is much to work with aside from bones and a few bits of buttons from their clothing according to the detective who went in there today."

"And then what happens?" he asked. "Will they bury them or close up the hole?"

"I'm not sure, but I will definitely let you know if you're interested," she said, digging her phone from her purse. "Here," she said.

"Make sure your phone number is listed as the best number to reach you. I'll call you and let you know what's going on when I hear."

Ron Adamson took the phone and confirmed his information.

"I would appreciate that," he said. "If they have any sort of burial services, I'd like to be there. It would be sort of an apology for what my great-grandfather did."

"I understand and I'll keep you updated," Joanna said. She got up to leave. "Thank you for letting me barge in on you again."

"I appreciate your keeping me informed," he said, opening the door for Joanna. He held her gaze for a moment. "Thank you."

"It's no problem," she said, placing her hand on his forearm briefly before walking out, the door closing behind her.

CHAPTER 20

ONE MONTH LATER

Joanna stood at the grave site in Oak Grove Cemetery with her children and three-month-old Iris slumbering in the baby carrier at Jim's feet. Even Julia took a day off to be there on a Tuesday. They were there to pay their respects to two former slaves who had the audacity to ask for wages and been killed for their efforts. The city had removed the bodies and carefully closed up the root cellar so no one would go poking around. The outer door of the room was sealed again, waiting for a possible renovation into an actual closet at some point in the future. The problem was no one wanted a 'haunted closet,' so sealed was the way it would remain for the foreseeable future.

The names of the two men found in the root cellar were never discovered, but all of the notes in the journal confirmed the assumptions that they were indeed workers on the tobacco farm who also worked in the house. The slave story seemed plausible, so the detectives decided to add it to their report and move on. The case was closed with only the formal burial to be conducted before they rested in peace.

The pastor from the First Congregational Church in West Haven agreed to provide a non-sectarian service at the graveside and everything else was either donated or funds were raised to cover what was needed. The funeral home donated their services to place the remains of the two men together in a simple casket that was paid for by a collection taken by the Library Board of Directors. The required vault in which to bury the casket was also paid for by the collection, and a small choir from West Haven High School showed up with their choir director to sing.

It was all respectful and very sweet. Nothing less than these two men deserved in Joanna's opinion.

As Joanna surveyed the group around the gravesite, she saw Ron Adamson was there, as promised, as was Buddy Lawson and all of the members of the Library's Board of Directors along with Celine. She was grateful for the investigations especially now that the Reference Room was quiet again; no more taps around the room and no more books left in weird places. The three detectives, Sal and Lucas and also shown up along with Sal's crew along with a scattering of other residents of West Haven, faces Joanna knew by site if not personally. In total there were about forty people standing at the graveside of two men they never knew. It was what made West Haven what it was; a caring place despite the squabbles and gossip this closeness sometimes produced. West Haven residents took care of their own, and sometimes other people as well.

Joanna was impressed with the little choir when it was their turn. They sang a beautiful rendition of *The Irish Blessing* which Joanna thought was perfect in the current situation. They were sending the two souls to Heaven to rest in peace, saying we will meet them again in another place at another time. It was the perfect ending to make up for two lives lost in tragic circumstances.

The last note rang clear through the cooling September air of the cemetery, the pastor thanked everyone for coming and the crowd dispersed. Joanna's family was silent for a moment before Iris woke up and began her little squeak for food that would soon become a wail if they didn't move forward and feed her soon.

"I guess that's our cue," Maggie said as Jim picked up the carrier.

"I was going to suggest the diner for lunch, but why don't you all swing by my house for lunch?" Joanna offered. "I'm sure I can scare up something or we can order in."

"I'm there," Maggie said. "I can't resist your coffee."

"Me, either," Jim said.

"Aren't you breastfeeding anymore?" Joanna asked trying not to sound like she was meddling.

"No, I had to give it up," Maggie replied. "This little one eats like a fiend and I wasn't making enough milk for her appetite!"

"Plus, this way I can take over the middle-of-the-night feedings for her," Jim said.

"I made a sweet son, there, didn't I?" Joanna said, .

"You certainly did," Maggie said, her smile at her husband was radiant.

"Okay, so let's go make a pot of coffee and start from there," Joanna said, leading the way to the cars.

"Did I hear coffee?" Buddy Lawson said as he walked up to Joanna.

"Yes!" Joanna said. "We're heading back to my house for some. Will you join us?"

"No thanks," he said. "I don't want to interrupt your family gathering. Besides, I need to get back to the office for a little while. Enjoy your time together!"

"We will, Buddy," she said. "Thank you for everything."

"No thank you," he said, still holding her outstretched hand. "If it weren't for you and Celine, we never would have found these two men."

"No worries," Joanna said. "I'm happy to help." The rest of her family had moved on to a polite distance while Joanna and Buddy Lawson chatted.

"I'll see you when I see you," Lawson said and walked on while Joanna met up with her family. She saw Ron Adamson walking ahead of them and thought better of going up to him. What did she really have to say aside from mindless chitchat anyway? He was probably better left with his thoughts.

Joanna had heard he confronted his nephew, Daniel, about the journal, but it was her understanding they had patched things up. In fact it was Daniel who went to retrieve the journal from the police when they were finished with it. He extracted a promise that its contents would not become fodder for discussion outside the detective squad, then returned it to his uncle with apologies if not regret. He told Joanna he was glad the story was out and the whole family could move forward from that dark time in their history.

As for the little boy, his soul was settled as well. It seemed as if he just wanted his presence known as a way of letting in the two men. Joanna found little else about him. She could only invent his story and know, through his revelations to her, that he was back with his mother. She only hoped there would be no more sounds from that space on the side of the library. Celine was already looking up shamans and other faith healers on which to call should the activity start up again, but so far, all was quiet in the library. No bumps or tapping in the Reference Room.

"Let's get moving, folks," she said, following her little crew back to the parking lot. A strong cup of coffee and maybe sandwiches were waiting back at her house. She would have to see what was in her fridge. Joanna would take the day off away from writing, unless she felt like it after the group left, and away from investigating any ghost-like situations. This was a day to enjoy her children and her granddaughter. It was clear you never knew how many days like this were in one's future and she wanted to enjoy every one of them.

The End

ACKNOWLEDGEMENTS

It isn't easy being a full-time author, but it is truly the best job in the world for me. I could not do it without the help of some people, so here are a few I need to thank. I am sure I am missing some people but know that you are much appreciated.

First, I want to thank my virtual assistant, Cindy Springsteen. Your review of my manuscript helped make it the best version possible. Your promotion skills help me do what I love to do – write!

My beta readers, or 'street team,' came out of the woodwork to answer my call for readers in advance of the launch. Thank you for your help!

Above all, I have to thank my husband and sons for putting up with the thrown-together dinners after a full day of writing, my closed door while I wrote, and all of the cheering on they gave me as I pursued my goal of this book series, a new genre for me. You are my everything.

Enjoy the journey,
Rosemary O'Brien

Thank you for reading GHOSTLY PASSAGE. If you would like to keep up with all of my new releases, sign up for my newsletter at www.AuthorRosemaryOBrien.com/

OTHER BOOKS UNDER THE NAME R.K. O'BRIEN:

Ghostly Command

OTHER BOOKS UNDER THE NAME ROSEMARY O'BRIEN:

First Saturday & Scraps: 2-Books

Best Pocket Parks of NYC – A guide to the 56 best pocket parks in New York City.

Facing Forward (Poetry)

Sometimes Try Is All There Is: Caregiving With Grace and Humor – A caregiver's guide to dealing with a loved one's illness with grace, humor and a little wackiness.

Manufactured by Amazon.ca
Bolton, ON